The Hospital for Bad Poets

Also
by
J. C. Hallman

The Chess Artist

The Devil Is a Gentleman

The Hospital for Bad Poets

J. C. HALLMAN

milkweed
editions

© 2009, Text by J. C. Hallman
All rights reserved. Except for brief quotations in critical articles or reviews, no part of this book may be reproduced in any manner without prior written permission from the publisher: Milkweed Editions, 1011 Washington Avenue South, Suite 300, Minneapolis, Minnesota 55415. (800) 520-6455
www.milkweed.org

Published 2009 by Milkweed Editions
Printed in the United States of America
Cover design by Brad Norr
Cover photo by Andy Kingsbury/Corbis
Author photo by Laura Migliorino
Interior design by Steve Foley
The text of this book is set in Lino Letter Roman.
09 10 11 12 13 5 4 3 2 1
First Edition

Please turn to the back of this book for a list of the sustaining funders of Milkweed Editions.

Library of Congress Cataloging-in-Publication Data

Hallman, J. C.
    The hospital for bad poets / J. C. Hallman.
        p. cm.
    Short stories.
    ISBN 978-1-57131-074-3 (pbk. : acid-free paper)
    I. Title
    PS3608.A5484H67 2009
    813'.6—dc22   2008047008

This book is printed on acid-free paper

THE HOSPITAL FOR BAD POETS

No more collective crusades, no more citizens, but wan and disabused individuals, still ready to answer the call of a utopia, though on condition that it come from *somewhere else*, on condition that they need not bother to conceive it themselves.

—E. M. Cioran

The
Hospital
for
Bad
Poets

THE EPIPHENOMENON

The average man is not what he used to be. At first, he thinks this is normal. The average is a function of time and one can reasonably expect to remain average only for so long. In history's current predicament the average man is slightly past his prime. He is fully aware of this. There is age and decay to consider. Yet when the average man wakes on a spring morning in a wet season his thought is this: *I am not what I used to be.*

The average man looks in the mirror more often than he cares to admit. Doing so this morning, he spots nothing that can account for the vaguely run-down feeling, not quite disease, not quite exhaustion, something more spectral and unaccountable. The average man consults his wife at such moments of doubt, as, though he is loath to admit it, her instincts in these matters tend to be better than his own.

"You're paranoid," she says. "That's so like you. That's your forte, your favorite thing. The only time I'm surprised is when you feel fine, which you should, obviously, more often. I imagine it's common for men of your age and disposition to think they are less than what they once were. Which does not mean there's nothing wrong with you. I've held that opinion for quite some time, actually. Rather, I expect that whatever phenomenon you are experiencing afflicts millions of men like yourself and perhaps even more."

The average man does not agree with his wife's diagnosis, but he remains quiet. He has been married long enough to know that she is not finished speaking. The meat is still to come. In recent years, the average man's wife has taken to wearing her bathrobe all day long. As well, she tends to favor expensive medications whose effect is supposed to be a pleasant mood but that actually leave her irritable. This does not strike the average man as particularly funny, only sad and untimely. His wife slowly lights a cigarette, nearly igniting one of the sleeves of her robe. She shrugs. "Go to the doctor."

"We're pleased," the GP says, two weeks later, two weeks in which the average man's malaise has not so much worsened as settled in, a growth slaloming the course of his spine. The GP leafs through page after page of test results. "You did quite well. You held up like a trooper. It didn't look like you were going to be able to sit still through some of those procedures, but you managed nicely. The results show it. Nothing exceptional, but that's what we hope for. We don't see that too often, actually. This is not that kind of facility. Everything is in the range we have come to expect."

"For a man my age?"

"For a man any age. We're really quite happy. We're still somewhat confused, of course. After all, you're here. But we're quite impressed."

"We," the average man says.

"Well," the GP smiles, "you and me."

The average man stares at the doctor's stethoscope, its

heavy hypnotic nugget dangling over his own heart.

"May I ask a personal question?" the GP says. "Granted, I am a doctor, so all of my questions are personal, but may I elevate the level of personalcy? How hard is it for you to achieve erection?"

"Not that hard."

"And how hard is it?"

"Well, you know, when . . . oh, I get it."

"Our little joke to break the ice. People don't often stop to consider the humor available through the medical industry. People focus on the negative. *A-, dys-, hypo-, hyper-*. It's a depressing vocabulary. Plus, you expect your doctor to talk over your head. You expect him to pulverize you with obscure theory and phlegmy Latin. It wouldn't be therapy without a complete language disconnect."

The average man glimpses graphs and minuscule analysis in his test results. The GP makes a note somewhere deep in the output.

"Well," he says, offering his hand, "we'll be hoping you feel better soon."

As a rule, the average man does not trust the GP because he lacks specialty. It's now altogether common for the average man to be aware of the lag in the dissemination of medical know-how, and the average man is certain that whatever ails him will require exhaustive study in a novel field. Effective treatment may take decades to trickle down to him. The average man resolves to confront his malaise by ignoring it—all evidence aside, the average man is still a believer in the healing power of self-will—and he reasons that in all likelihood it is the divergence from strict routine that accounts for his dysfunction. As it happens, it is just his morning habit of coffee and newspaper that brings to him the advertisement that he is at once certain will lead to remedy. He burns his tongue taking in the words.

Feeling rundown?
Otherwise apathological?
Conventional life sciences at a loss?
Call United Statisticians for a free evaluation.

"Ouch," the average man says.

"Are you all right?" his wife says, refilling his cup.

Generally, the average man considers the double entendre of such questions only fleetingly, perhaps unconsciously. "Do you have to make it so hot?"

"Classic," she says, shaking her head. "Run-of-the-mill. It's coffee," she explains.

But there is no phone number attached to the advertisement. The average man pinches the oniony pages of the phone book, but oddly finds only an address, deep in the city. He calls in sick from work, which may very well be the case. The average man kisses his wife as he leaves, confident for some reason that whatever he has isn't catching.

The building had been erected by a powerhouse corporate entity long since extinct, the structure since invaded by a variety of unlikely enterprises. A woman trained exotic reptiles on the first floor, secret psychological research was conducted on the second. Civilian attachés for military intelligence held quiet think tanks on the third, a flying saucer cult lived year-round on the fourth. And so on up through the heart of the building, only the window washers witness to it all, ascending bimonthly like lazy souls past a succession of bizarre industry.

The average man double-checks the fly of his slacks in the elevator, as he is wont. He exits on the eighth floor, finds the door of United Statisticians, pushes it aside quietly. A small waiting room can accommodate half a dozen. The average man tends to approach receptionists cautiously in a polite attempt to defuse the nearly imperceptible sexual charge in these encounters, and as he does so now the young woman, hair coiffed and mouth neatly painted, and planted in her chair as though the slightest curvature of spine would give her pain, does not notice him and continues a pencil drawing that appears to have been occupying her for some time. The receptionist is left-handed. The average man is charmed by this. Her drawing is that of an eye as large as a palm. The eye is blurry but correct, and nearly complete as she adds a lash or two with quick turns of her crimped hand.

"It's very nice," he says, the only reply the average man uses in responding to others' attempts at art.

"Oh." The receptionist jumps and slides the eye into a desk drawer. "You frightened me."

"I'm sorry."

She is quite lovely, really. It is not something he is keen to admit, but the soft charge of social routine conducted with strangers is the most rewarding form of intimacy the average man knows. Although it's been several decades since the average man wore a hat with regularity, he finds that as he stands before the receptionist his fingers fondle the brim of an imaginary bowler suspended in front of his groin.

The receptionist gathers herself, dabs at her coif, and threads her slender fingers. "What are you looking for? Cosmetic irradiation is one floor up, sex catering is one floor down. Stairs are around the corner, facilities are at the end of the hall."

"I think I'm in the right place."

She looks at him more closely now, eyes pinching so that for a moment they resemble the eye in her drawing. Contemplative, searching. "Oh, I'm sorry," she says. "I didn't realize. So many people get lost. It's an odd building, you see, and—" Now she seems to recognize something in him, something that takes her quite by surprise. She adopts a more delicate tone. "You're not feeling—yourself, are you?"

His simple presence there has tilted his hand. The average man is embarrassed as when someone he does not know calls him by name.

"Not really."

The receptionist reaches for a phone and presses a heavy button that lights at her touch. "Alert the Maestro," she says to the receiver. She cradles the handset again and turns back to him. "I'm so sorry. I've botched things. I was given several weeks of training, and I really did have it down quite expertly. A number of other girls stumbled over the script, or just

didn't have the exact look they were looking for, they said, and they remarked on my progress and speaking skills, but now it's not at all clear that I was the right candidate for—"
She sees a pleading look in the average man's eyes, sees that he is admiring her, and the smile she produces when she cuts herself off is not quite flirtation but, the average man concludes, an acknowledgment of romantic potential. It quickly passes, and the receptionist puts on the air of an actor before delivering a speech she was presumably supposed to deliver initially.

"We need a life not correlated with death," she says. "Health not liable to illness. Good that will not perish, good that flies beyond the good of nature." She smiles, pleased with her performance. "You may have a seat. Someone will be with you shortly."

The Statistician appears in a doctor's white coat, holding a file folder over his chest as though to block a bullet. He is a smallish man with glasses. He extends a palm to invite the average man back into the office. "Welcome," he says. "Please." The Statistician is quite excited, as though the average man is of status and fame, which of course he is not. The Statistician introduces himself, but the average man has never been particularly good at remembering names.

The Statistician leads them to an examination room. White cupboards stand against white walls, chrome devices with crooked elbows lurk about a curling dentist's chair.

"You saw the ad, didn't you?" the Statistician says.

"Yes, just this morning."

The Statistician claps his hands together before him, where they stick as though to trap a fly. He shakes his head in happy disbelief. As with the receptionist, the average man senses that the Statistician's outburst is a digression from protocol. Somewhat overwhelmed, the average man fits himself into the reclined socket of the dentist's chair.

"Please forgive me," the Statistician says. "But, you see, the advertisement was my idea, perhaps my largest contribution to the project. There was a great deal of doubt about this idea, even within our small circle of confederates. I was the subject of hushed insults, of which some believed I was unaware. But of course I knew there would be talk. Still, I proceeded, and the advertisement brought you here, so it's validation for me, don't you see?"

"Congratulations," the average man says.

The Statistician initiates another vigorous handshake. "Thank you. My, I can't tell you. Our circle has been subject to a number of attacks from outside, in some cases from quite well placed sources. These attacks had begun to have a certain effect, and, to be honest, it had gotten to the point where some members of our little conglomerate had begun to question whether you did, in fact, *exist*."

Charmingly, the average man's response to confusion is to repeat established information. "I saw the ad when I was drinking my coffee," he says.

The Statistician smiles. "Perfect. Top of the curve. Now, I'm sure you're quite curious as to what we're up to here, yes? My. How to begin. You think you've prepared for a thing, and when the thing arrives you realize you're entirely ready but for the easiest of first steps." He taps his lower lip. "You're not feeling yourself, correct? You feel unwell, off, and that's what's brought you here. Let's start with this. The Greeks were the first to offer a model of disease that went beyond the ontological. Health is harmony. Disturbance of equilibrium is disease. Agreed?"

"That's what I have, I think," the average man says. He is pleased the conversation has turned to his ailment. The plastic cushion of the chair begins to mold to his form.

"Gosh, if only those old theories applied, eh?" the Statistician says. "Wouldn't that be nice. Now it seems inevitable to us that disease would be understood first as either exaggeration or deficiency. How quaint! But I ask you. What about the anomaly that does not produce deformity? It's just that easy to confuse variety with dysfunction."

"I feel sick," the average man says.

"Of course you do. What other word would you have for it?"

"I want to get better."

"Quite right. The normal state of the body is the state one wishes to reestablish. This is textbook. But press just a little and it stops seeming so simple. Answer honestly now. Do you want to get better because therapeutics has determined it is a good goal, or because you think it's normal that therapeutics aim at getting better? Or think of it this way. What are your symptoms?"

The average man stares.

"You see? The standard diagnostic procedure. In medicine

it is the sick man who decides when he is sick, and it is the sick man who decides when he is well again. But where is the evidence of your disease?"

"I don't feel normal."

The Statistician rears back and throws a hand into the air. "Ha! That's a whole other can of worms. Normal in what way exactly? Are human traits normal because they occur frequently? Or do they occur frequently because they are normal? If everyone gets sick then illness is quite normal, isn't it?"

"You're not a doctor, are you?" the average man says.

"Sure I am. This is a hospital. Nurse! Bring the mind cures! Bring the leeches! Bring the chemotherapy!" The Statistician spasms with laughter. He nibbles a knuckle to stifle it, but it is persistent as a cough. "I'm sorry. Consider a blocked artery. Is it still an artery? Or is it an obstruction? Is a necrotic cell still a cell? A man who dies is no longer a man, is he? He's a corpse. In medicine, opinions are formed on palpation, interpretation. We are outside of science. Whether a tumor is malign or benign is a question for philosophy."

"So this is a lab?"

The Statistician squints at the ceiling. "I might have predicted you'd say that. What else could this be? Call it a clinic."

"A clinic."

"Now do you see the problem of the quantitative model of disease? Any range of intensity is labeled sick. The average is synonymous with mediocrity. Well, I think it must be apparent to you by now that once we rejected

this as fallacy you were bound to sense a change." The
Statistician scans the average man's eyes. "I see you don't
understand. Think of this. An animal is normal within its
habitat. But what happens when its habitat changes? In
the new habitat, it's no longer normal. Quote. Pathological
phenomena are expressions of change in the relationship
between organism and environment. Unquote. Now what of
man? Man creates his environment. And this environment
includes that which he understands of himself. Thus, the
average man will continue to feel well only as long as no
one successfully challenges that which defines average.
Once the old theories have been struck down, he will begin
to feel less than average. He will feel *below* average."

"That's it," the average man says. "That's what I feel."

"Now do you see why we are excited? Your illness is
evidence of progress. You have been ontologically jolted, my
friend! The Maestro is better at explaining, but one way of
thinking of it is this: you were sicker before."

"I felt fine."

"That doesn't matter, of course. And now that you feel off?
Someone else has woken this morning feeling shiny and
chipper. Of course, you want us to cure you. Even the average
man has an understanding of health. You want to be well
again. You want to be yourself. You want us to do it. But I ask
you, good sir—my God—how?"

Honestly, the Statistician's words, to the extent he can
follow them, are not wholly unrewarding for the average
man. The average man secretly suspects his entire life that
he is the subject of some distant experiment, that civilization

itself is a ruse constructed so that truth can be deduced from his decisions. The average man is a secret solipsist, and now through his terror he feels excitement.

"Who is the Maestro?"

"The Maestro is preparing. We—well, I, I suppose I should say—are quite proud of him. He's a revolutionary. We—you and I—we're both honored by our association with him." The Statistician steps toward the door. "I should help him with his preparations. He'll be coming to speak with you before the performance."

"The performance?"

The Statistician smiles. "It will be just a minute," he says.

✛

The average man sits in the room drolly for a time. He pushes aside the curtain over a window only to find that it is not a window but a compartment with a fluorescent bulb masquerading as one. The Statistician has left behind the file folder that is presumably the record United Statisticians has compiled on the average man, but when he opens it all that flutters to the floor is a lunch receipt from a nearby deli. The average man jerks upright when the door opens again and the Maestro enters the room.

There is no mistaking him. The Maestro tugs the cuff-linked sleeves of a tuxedo shirt to their proper length as he crosses the threshold. He has long white clean hair, and a perfect white beard. The tails of his jacket follow him into the room, lie against his calves. Once he has properly arrived, he

shudders once head-to-toe to allow the tuxedo to settle about
his entire frame. The Statistician follows him into the room.

"Have they begun to assemble?" the Maestro says,
speaking through his entrance. "Someone has contacted
Forchet, yes? He's a twit, but I want him here. Did you read
what he delivered in Vienna last week? Bah! What about
Lautier? Not the Canadian one, the French one. I'll show him
numerical models. What about the Old Man? Have we sent
for the Old Man? It's nothing without the Old Man."

The Statistician smoothes the shoulder of the Maestro's
jacket in an intimate touch. They are both quite absorbed in
the Maestro's speech.

"The limousine is on its way, Maestro," the Statistician says.

"Good." The Maestro exhales and finally cannot think of
anything more to do. It is boredom that brings him to look
about the room and lay his eyes on the average man. He
freezes. He squints as though to induce a trance. The Maestro
flows forward a step, offering his hand, and the Statistician
scurries along behind.

"Ah. It's odd to see him in the flesh, isn't it?" the Maestro
says, and even though their hands are clasped his words
are not meant for the average man. "My, the feeling. To
confront your epiphenomenon. Is it more like the pride of a
father whose son has grown, or the artist whose vision has
realized?" The Maestro smiles and laughs out loud. He grabs
the average man by both shoulders and squares him. "Before
modern medicine, the average man was understood as an
expression of God's will. You might as well cast bones. But
now, the average man is an expression of *our* will."

The average man is naturally curious and uncomfortable when people discuss him as though he is not present. But at the same time he is quite susceptible to the awe of men with stature, to social hierarchy in general, and thus he can neither adequately express his discomfort nor convey the authority or self-will of which he is occasionally capable.

"What's going on here?" he says.

"It's funny," the Maestro says with a grin. "If he was an automaton I would say he was remarkably lifelike." Behind him, the Statistician can't help a fiendish smirk. The Maestro's expression now changes, like a parent putting on a pleasant face to address a child. "Medicine is linked to the whole of culture, wouldn't you agree?" he says to the average man.

In situations in which it is not clear that one need reply, the average man's policy is to remain silent. The Maestro only waits, and the Statistician leans between them.

"Maestro, if I may, we spoke at some length earlier— quite the little exchange, really—and although it's certainly a premature assessment, I'm not quite sure that he is capable of—"

"Hogwash!" The Maestro releases the average man and points emphatically at the ceiling. "The man who feels sick is obviously mistaken in thinking that he knows why he feels this way. But it does not follow that his theory, too, is in error. The average man is perfectly capable of understanding."

The Maestro paces the room a bit, rubbing a meaty palm over his hairy mouth. He turns back to the average man.

"Therapeutics was at first a religious, magical activity. You know—witch doctors, shamans? Disease is evil, health is good. Health and disease fought over man the way Good and Evil battled for the world. Truth be told, we're all witch doctors in retrospect: Paracelsus believed he had found the elixir of life, Van Helmont identified health with salvation, and Stahl himself believed in original sin. But here's the thing. When we denied the ontological conception of disease, we denied the *possibility of evil*."

The average man climbs back into the dentist's chair.

The Maestro follows, frustrated. "Surely you must acknowledge that the average man knows he is average only in a world where all are average. Otherwise, he feels special, singled out. Perhaps he even feels unreasonably oppressed or used. He begins to suspect that he is not average at all. He becomes a tragic fool. Ignorant and browbeaten. But can one innocently know that one is innocent? No one who is good is aware of his being good, and no one who is healthy knows that he is healthy."

The Maestro pauses to see if his words have found purchase. The average man can only nod weakly.

"Bah! You're like the rest of them! Don't you see? The abnormal is not what is not normal. It constitutes *another* normal. To be sick is to live another life. Health is organic innocence. Innocence must be lost for the sake of knowledge. The sick man advances knowledge of the average man. To be ill is to be wise."

"You did this to me," the average man says.

"Notice his verb choice," the Maestro says. "Quote. The sick man is not abnormal because of the absence of a norm but because of an incapacity to be average. Unquote." The

Statistician nods and jots a note.

"Do you know *Everyman?*" the Maestro asks the average man. "Of course you don't. How extremely unlikely that you would. Morality play. John Skot. Early sixteenth century. Perhaps oversimplified for its uneducated audience, but quite popular in its day. Everyman is the embodiment of mankind. At the beginning of the play, Everyman has become so enamored of his wealth that he has forgotten the father in heaven and his own mortality. God sends Death to guide Everyman on a tour of his vanity. Everyman tries to bribe Death, then agrees to a journey to confront various virtues: Knowledge, Beauty, Goodness, and whatnot. A clunky tool to be sure. But the message is more interesting than the method. Everyman comes to think of his odyssey as a disease that needs remedying. He is advised to go to the priesthood to receive a sacramental 'ointment.' There he is told:

> *For the blessed sacraments pure and benign*
> *He beareth the keys and thereof have the cure*
> *For man's redemption it is ever sure*
> *Which God for our soul's medicine*
> *Gave us out of his heart with great pain.*

"You see? God becomes the metaphysician to cure Everyman's sin! And at the end, it's not an angel who appears to advise the audience as to the play's moral reckoning. It's a doctor. A doctor!"

The Maestro lays a hand on the average man's shoulder, kneading it like a lover. "It is every scientist's hope that his hypothesis can change the world. My friend, you are my evidence, my truth, my epiphenomenon. I have waited for you. Our own audience is gathering. Are you ready?"

✚

The average man is left alone to prepare. In the chair he experiences an odd sensation of vertigo, and he lifts himself upright in its cup. He feels sicker than when he arrived, yet at the same time he senses that he may be on the cusp of that which will assuage him. He is anxious. It is the receptionist who retrieves him, knocking first and peeking at him from behind the jamb.

"Hello," the average man says.

She enters the room carefully, schoolgirlish and shy. She puts her feet together and shrugs. "I suppose this is awfully obvious, isn't it? Sending me in here to fetch you along. Rather transparent. If I had my say I'd say even the average man can see through such a ridiculous ploy. I would! I'd say, the average man isn't nearly the dupe you think he is. I've seen one or two in my time, so I should know. Besides, being average only means that the average man makes average mistakes, and if the world's got any real problems it's that exceptional men make exceptional mistakes. And it's just those jokers who turn into monsters behind closed doors! Hm!"

The receptionist nods once, and the average man can barely contain the swoon of his heart. The receptionist holds his stare.

"I hate to do this. But there are some things I'm supposed to tell you before we go."

"What things?"

She looks to the ceiling for her recital. "Quote. Even a sick man can carry on the moral warfare. He can will his attention away from his own future. He can train himself in indifference to his own suffering. He can cultivate cheerful manners and be silent about his misery. Does not such a man inhabit the loftiest of planes? Is he not a high-hearted freeman and no pining slave? Unquote." She lowers her head and breathes. "And now I'm just supposed to take you to the auditorium. But—well—how do you *feel*?"

"Queasy."

"They said you'd say that. They said it's normal."

"They said a lot," the average man says.

"Oh, dear!" the receptionist says. She steps forward to embrace him, and he stands to enter her arms. "I'm not supposed to do this at all."

One hand the receptionist lays into the small of the average man's back, the other cups his skull as though he is an infant. The average man pulls her forward, a palm for each distinct shoulder blade, and he feels himself become aroused, as will tend to happen. They remain pressed for several seconds, then the receptionist pulls away. Her eyes have begun to water, and she flaps a stiff palm by her face to stem the tears.

"Oh my, look at me. Not very professional, and this only my second formal position!" She steps back a pace to assume a new pose of formality. "Without the sacrifice of the average man, is it not surprising that health exists at all? Please follow me."

She leads him further into the building, out from the hallways of the clinic decorated with prints of barns and flowers, into tile-walled passages that twist and curve, and finally through a pair of swinging doors splotched with square windows. Beyond is a half flight of stairs; the dismal corridor continues at the bottom. The Maestro's voice is clear in the passage before it arrives at its terminus, a door marked STAGE. They stop and lean close to listen.

"Disease!" the Maestro bellows. "Has there ever been a means of investigation so rich in result? Illness, my gracious colleagues, is an experiment of the most subtle order! What is a symptom without context or background? What is complication apart from what it complicates? Have we not come to learn, my dear friends, that to define disease we must dehumanize it? Is it not obvious now that man is the least important element of sickness?

"Medicine needs objective pathology. But research that destroys its subject is hardly objective! The laboratory itself is a pathological environment. From this, researchers—some of you here today—claim to draw conclusions bearing the weight of norms. But I ask you. When a drosophila with wings gives birth to a drosophila without wings, are we confronted with pathological fact? Does the latter feel it is less than its ancestor? Does it feel sick? At every moment the possibilities within us are endless. It takes disease to reveal them. Today, we see the results of an experiment conducted in the purest of laboratories—life itself! Our subject came to us. The very fact that he calls himself sick is our failure to disprove."

There follows a great murmuring as the hidden audience comes alive. The average man and the receptionist share the surprise. Judging from the vibration, the audience may well number a thousand. The receptionist squints consolingly. From this the average man deduces that he will be introduced soon. She places a hand on his shoulder and tilts her head as though to see deeper into his eyes. A kiss at this moment is the instinct of the average man. But though she is close enough that he can feel her breath on his lips, the average man does not move toward her. Generally speaking, he thinks, the Maestro may be right that he does not know that he is average. That the average man secretly believes he is more than average may be the prototype of prayer. It is a sad thought, but a universal one. And was there not comfort there? The average man is simple, but not a prisoner. He may tend toward stoicism and timidity, he may lack significant foresight and wherewithal, but was there not at least one great moment in the lives of all men, when even an average man could transcend expectation and cry his name aloud?

"Friends! Friends!" the Maestro calls beyond the door, silencing the room. "If you do not believe, you will meet him in but a moment. But a question first. Do we not know that the healthy organism does more than simply maintain itself? Does it not attempt to realize its nature? We have the obligation to interfere with ourselves, to vulgarize our genius."

A voice from the audience interrupts. "You're quoting Canguilhem!"

"And he's quoting Quetelet!" the Maestro calls. "And Comte! And Broussais! This is what we do. We borrow, we build, we tear down. Life gambles against growing entropy!"

A number of voices call out. "What of Commonplace Man . . . Ideal Man . . . Prevalent Man . . . Regular Man . . . Representative Man."

"Enough! It is time for him to appear."

There is a pause beyond the door, and the average man sees the receptionist wet her lips, preparing to deliver some element of her script. Her hand moves toward the knob of the stage door. The average man reaches for her wrist before she can betray him.

"My colleagues," the Maestro says, "my collaborators and competitors alike. I give you proof!"

"Help me," the average man whispers.

His breath moves her hair. Even the skin of her wrist is feverish.

"Come," she says. "Hurry!"

They rush back up the passage, holding hands. They pass again through the swinging doors and along new corridors. Their heartbeats accelerate with their footsteps, and she leads him to an exit behind a thick velvet curtain. Beyond is an abyss of stairs.

"Come with me," the average man says. "I love you."

"My dearest," the receptionist says, "we only think that we love. What we love are ideas." She takes both his hands. "Our troubles lie too deep for that cure. The fact that we can be ill at all is what perplexes us. But do not fear. It is the patient who decides when he has returned to normalcy. The essential thing is to have been raised from near death. To have had a narrow escape. You are fine. You will feel yourself soon enough. Now go!"

She nods him toward the stairs and disappears behind the curtain. The average man stands still a moment. He is sad, but he must admit that he has begun to feel better. He breathes in the dank air of the stairwell and feels it process inside of him, begin its industrious distribution. The average man these days is well aware of how his organs work; he understands his own normal functioning. And now he descends through the building, past a school for mimes and sad circus clowns, past a cryogenics storage warehouse, past a bottling center for a pink elixir that cures all ails, and emerges at last to a new world caught in spring downpour, fat droplets falling hard and shattering, an inconvenience to be sure but quite normal for that time of year.

ETHAN: A LOVE STORY

My parents' home sat inside a gated community called Sky
Meadow, a set of forty builder-designed mansions sprinkled
over a topographical elevation as neat as a cupcake. Sky
Meadow was protected at its base by a gatehouse and a
team of geriatric guards in gray uniforms who controlled the
white tube arm that blocked passage into the community.
The arm wouldn't really stop anybody, but there was a
hydraulic bollard beneath the pavement as well, an explosive
mechanism that would fire metal rods into the engine
compartment of undesirable vehicles.

Sky Meadow was veined with the green wending swaths of
a golf course, and my parents' home sat on the last of these,
the eighteenth fairway, the home hole. They had furnished
their house with a stratum of knickknacks that described their
five-decade-long ascent from poverty. The three-dollar bowl
that my mother had once broken and glued back together, bit
by bit, was as precious to her as her baby doll, a collectible
figurine she had won at auction. My father kept on his desk his
beaten old slide rule—his BS in physics, nearly half a century
old, had been more than enough to make him a successful
corporate inventor—but alongside it was a bust of himself that
he had once commissioned on a whim. My parents thought of

themselves as retired, and their main activity now consisted of occupying that weird collection: the odd bits of fantastic art of the truly wealthy, the framed family portraits that charted their passage through middle class, and the kitsch—a variety of plastic Mickey Mouse figurines, a cheap oil lamp once used for actual light—set about like displays of the primitive culture from which their kind had evolved.

When I went home for Christmas that year, I hadn't ever seen my six-year-old nephew, Ethan. But even this was a point of disagreement for me and my family—my parents and brother and sister and their spouses—a group who had decided to respond to the world's basic intricacy so differently from me that just recognizing myself in them, in their mannerisms and bad habits, made me kind of lonely. Nobody could figure out why I had turned out so differently; it might have been a mutation I was born with. I tended to avoid family gatherings, as useless argument always ruled the day. I was still unmarried—that was surely part of it—and I was the youngest, too, though none of us was still young.

My sister-in-law insisted that I had met Ethan when he was nine months old, and my mother swore to an even more recent meeting. But the truth was I had never been within three states of the boy. Every family has its odd uncle—for the last generation it had been my Uncle Billy, who had become a monk—and it had been several years since I realized that I had become the odd uncle of the new generation. I didn't forget the birthdays of my nieces and nephews, I ignored them. I failed entirely in slithering those insipid greetings into their sleeves and weighing them down with crisp bills for toys or candy. I was an utter failure as a relative. Or so the family would have concluded, and perhaps they weren't wrong about that. I've given up trying to articulate the etymology of the dreads to which I seem to be prone, but it was precisely a sense of failure that had sent me home that year in the first place. A malevolent mood had struck, so disturbing that even the thought of family seemed a comfort. I agreed to go home. For, despite all the scuffles and ricocheting ridicule, despite my established unwholesomeness, my family still wished to see *me*. This was an intricate puzzle, like the little hokey bits of mangled wire, which, in their dismantling, are meant to make a diverting amusement and are often exchanged as presents at family Christmases. I didn't know why they wanted me—perhaps for the opportunity to turn the other cheek.

The sense of enclosure to my parents' home, at least for my mother, had resulted in an insidious agoraphobia—often she would not step outside the house for four or five days at a stretch—and, like each of the last several houses the family had lived in (there were thirteen in all), this one had come outfitted with a sophisticated security alarm device. The windows and doors at home were all wired; infrared beams latticed the rooms at night. The exact technology had grown more ominous from home to home, but the alarm paraphernalia, whatever it was, came to be known in the family cant as "the system." We children had first been given special keys for the system, then were forced to memorize codes. One false alarm, long ago, had brought to the house a helicopter and half a dozen police cruisers running red light and siren.

I came home that year equipped with an early present from a beautiful lady friend. That was how I thought of her—my beautiful lady friend, married to another. The gift was a green sweater, and I swooned when my friend told me it would ignite the color in my eyes. I wore it home with a kind of dumb hope that it would armor me against the volleys I expected from my family—my own private security system. The general anxiety of being home took added jolt when, just two days into the sentence, I made the fool mistake—indeed, it confirmed that somehow I had wandered onto intellectual flatland—of washing the sweater and throwing it into the tumble dryer, which was set to HIGH/COTTON. The lint shield felted over like a pool table. The sweater came out in perfect miniature. I presented it to Ethan, whom it now fit perfectly. I tugged the collar over his head and told him the sweater had come from a lovely girl. The boy's eyes tested this, and he decided to take a chance. "I like pretty girls," he said. "They make my eyes turn to hearts."

Ethan and I fell in love.

Ethan was a bright boy, dark-haired and dark-complexioned, and as he was now the youngest member of our unit—the only one who still believed in Santa Claus—he behaved with the requisite hyperactivity, frantic pleas for attention from us adults and those teenage children passing themselves off as adults by joining the family table and waiting for the moment when their experience would let them chime in. Ethan was too young for that transition and knew it. So instead he would stalk us all from across the room, so that my mother would flutter her eyes to detach herself from whatever thought she'd been having and announce, "What's that noise? I heard a noise! Roger, did you turn on the system?" Ethan would giggle and pop out from behind the grandfather clock. Or he would turn sets of track lights off and on, or up and down if there was a dimmer switch, so that my brother or sister might ask loudly whether the house was haunted, and the phantom giggling would sound again. We returned to our loveless talk after these interruptions, and Ethan returned to the activity that kept him occupied the vast bulk of the time. This was his video game device, transported from his home in Florida and played on a television in the downstairs guest quarters. He spent hours with the gadget. Its complicated instrument of interactivity, a handheld controller pad with toggles and triggers and buttons, was for him as familiar a device for communicating his orientation to the world as were his legs or fingers. He preferred games targeted at adults, stories of mayhem and bloodlust, American valor transported to a future where the slaughter of aliens offended no one.

His favorite of the moment—surely about to be displaced by Santa's team of programmers—was called Halo, the name of an imaginary spaceborne ship. The bad guys were called the Covenant, animal-like men and robots. The boy, oblivious to the game's religious subtext—the sound track was Gregorian chant—focused on damage. He destroyed heavy machinery, murdered at will, and generally found expression for a child's amorality. He rarely played the actual game, though he did sit fixed through the story line that held the whole thing together. The boy simply inhabited Halo, the character he became for its duration. Even when he wasn't in the game—when he was neither haunting my parents' comfortable home nor finding his eyes turned to hearts by pretty girls—he spoke in quotations from its script. "I'm too pretty to die," he might say at a quiet dinner of tender scallops, citing some madman soldier. "You want some of this? Come on, Sarge. That's what *I'm* talking about. I'm too pretty to die."

If all houses are museums of personal archaeology, then my parents' house was even more—a cultural cross section of the Dream, the fantasy my parents had executed so well. It took me until I was an adult to understand that, all those years, my mother's alarm system had actually kept us trapped inside. Open a door somewhere in that house and no matter where you were you heard the beeps registering the possible intrusion, data transmitting to the security firm's log of trespasses. The system had been born of my mother's fear, but it had long since amounted to a transfer of angst—I felt claustrophobic in that house. It gave me the creeps. So on this particular junket east I took up the habit of leaving frequently to walk through the pine woods adjacent to Sky Meadow's golf course. The links were empty; the chill had scared off the last of the golfers a month before. The fairways themselves had frozen over. The expensive grass crunched loudly underfoot, and I left trails like the footprints of a ghost.

I am prone to loneliness, so I was pleased when Ethan, a day after he inherited my sweater, asked if he could join me. The family tensed at this request. How to protect the boy from his sordid uncle's influence? How to reject the request without trompling over the battery of politeness and common sense the family had crafted into its version of etiquette? They wanted me present, but they certainly didn't want my influence spread about. They must have thought of my journey home as a kind of inoculation for the teenagers, political homeopathy. I told Ethan that I would be glad for his company, but that he needed to ask permission. The boy complied by simply turning his head to the others. This produced the room's discomfort, and the family responded with a vocabulary of twitchings and shiftings. There were too many of them to just say no. Ethan was baffled by the delay, but waited silently for the adults to catch up and grant a grudging approval. The following interval spent clothing the boy against the weather might as well have been an effort to insulate him against nefarious dogma.

The stillness at the onset of winter stops time, or at least slows it, as though the cold has shriveled the works. It was morning still, but the dew of the night had frozen in midair and dropped down across Sky Meadow like a sheet of cellophane. Even the wasted space of the golf course felt like wilderness compared to the prison of the house. Ethan and I rejoiced in a sense of escape, and from here we could see how Sky Meadow was poised between the steeple of the downtown church and the flat roofs of the strip malls, studded with exhaust fans and air-conditioning units. The boy bounced along as a fat mound

of goose down and bunched wool, but thought of it as body
armor from his video game, chunky Kevlar. He immediately
scrounged from the underbrush a gunlike stick, branches
protruding like stocks or magazines, and shoved it up into
his armpit. "Come on, Sarge," Ethan said. "Move it up there,
Jenkins. I've got contact on the motion sensors—keep it tight."

I dug around among some limbs until Ethan indicated a
branch as thick as a baseball bat. I took it up, dooming a family
of phosphorescent grubs. I lodged the branch under my arm.

"That's a rocket launcher," Ethan said.

"You bet it is," I said, patting the barrel.

The boy grimaced. "You don't hold it like that." He clean-
jerked his own rifle up onto his shoulder and balanced it.
"Like this."

"I see. Like a bazooka."

"A what?"

"It's an old kind of gun."

Ethan shook his head and swaggered forward, in character,
his breath showing from his nose. "That's an AR-15 rocket-
assist grenade launcher. It can fire armor-piercing shells
against tanks. You're packing a ton o' fun there, soldier."

"I understand, sir." I settled the branch more firmly on
my shoulder to show it new respect. "Am I Sarge, or am I
Jenkins?" I said.

"Jenkins gets killed."

"Gotcha. And who are you?"

"I'm still Ethan," Ethan said. He took a step out into the
woods, creeping across the crisp needles that made the
forest's carpet. "*I'm too pretty to die*," he whispered.

I don't think a child can truly have a conversation at six years of age. They have the tools, the words and the grammar, and they fake it well, but a six-year-old is still stuck at monomania and all they can believe in with certainty is themselves. Fantasies—video games or Santa Claus—are every bit as real as that which can be felt or touched. Childhood is the lack of a value distinction between fact and fantasy. The only real use of conversation is to pry the two apart.

Ethan and I found the Covenant in the woods. We rooted them out and massacred them for their violent manners and heathen ideologies. Ethan used "Choochoochoochoochoo," for the sound effect of his assault rifle, and corrected me when I tried "bangBang!" for the rocket launcher. We coordinated our attack on the unsuspecting golf course. We ran the Covenant over and suffered only the loss of Private Jenkins. When we were done, when we had crisscrossed the stand of trees and our victory was a fact on the ground, I sat down against a stump and tipped back my imaginary helmet.

"Lieutenant Ethan?" I said.

"Yeah?"

"It's wrong to kill, isn't it? I mean for real?"

Ethan's eyes wandered off into the woods where he could still see the blood-lathered forms of our victims. He searched his memory for a prerecorded reply to my question, some macho aphorism. He shrugged, but I pretended not to see.

"Hm?"

He tilted his head. "This is just for fun. It's not real, Uncle C—." He tossed his rifle, his stick, onto the frozen ground. "See? It's not even the real *game*."

✚

Ethan and I became inseparable at that point. He demanded
that I sit next to him at dinners, he pulled out chairs for
me, he pounced into my lap or onto my back, he knocked
lightly on the door when I took naps or was in the bathroom.
He touched me whenever he could, as though the cushion
of flesh was a sufficient emotional umbilicus. The others
became jealous. They who had carefully monitored his
difficult birth, they who had followed his growth with four-
by-sixes magneted to their refrigerators, they who had sent
boxed treats and gifts for holidays when gatherings proved
impractical, they who had fulfilled all the obligations of
relatives—where was their reward for commitment and hard
work? Why did this odd uncle deserve the boy's affections?
They did not discuss this, as it was a failing they would rather
not admit, but it was a thought as common as a faith. Even
Ethan seemed aware of it and began conducting our romance
in secret. When the family was gathered on the opposing
sofas of the living room, verifying the futility of debating the
sanctity of embryonic life, for example, or calculating the
proper reaction to hostile nation-states, Ethan would walk up
stealthily and whisper in my ear, *"Uncle C—, would you come
downstairs with me?"* He meant that I should come play Halo
with him, the real Halo. The rest of the family took a dim
view of the game's violent nature. But it was hypocrisy. As it
happened, that Christmas our entire nation was poised on
the brink of military imperialism—the republic was casually

in favor of the slaughter of thousands of innocents to justify the removal of an unruly dictator a couple of continents over. The family flicked a hand and argued for war. It was just, the threat was real, and there was nothing else to do. The violence of the video game was distasteful to them, but the real thing was palatable, even delectable. But I didn't make the point. It meant I had Ethan to myself.

Ethan taught me how to use the controller pads—they were tricky—and we each took a character. Somehow, he split the television screen in half so that we had separate subjective views. The first time we entered the game's broad arena, we just slaughtered the aliens for a while. I slowly grew accustomed to Halo's map, its obstacles and trenches and structures. But Ethan bored quickly. Before long, he sauntered his character up beside mine, raised his weapon, and fired. My screen fizzled into hibernation mode. In Ethan's view, my character showed a fist-sized exit wound and a haze of atomizing blood pixels. I clutched my chest and fell. Ethan hurried forward to harvest my ammunition. The boy giggled.

"I *got* you, Uncle C—."

Resurrection was a toggle away. My screen fluttered back to its intimate first person. I scanned for Ethan. He hovered over my old dead form. I scrolled quickly through my armory of weapons and chose the self-loading assault shotgun meant for close quarters. I loaded, leveled the thing at my nephew's back, and sprayed his shoulder blades. He buckled and bled and began to limp away. I discharged the shotgun twice more, until he groaned and fell and his blood colored the ground. Beside me, Ethan laughed uncontrollably. Our legs touched, and in the moment before his own reincarnation he laid his head softly against my shoulder. Then he revived himself, and I used my toggles to weave through the blocky landscape, Ethan's projectiles swishing past me in the little lasers of tracer rounds.

Over the next several days, the Covenant stood by as Ethan and I devastated each other. The boy might find the game's elusive minigun and administer its lead enema. Or I would stumble across the flamethrower and crisp my nephew head to toe. "I'm too pretty to die," I told Ethan once, as I sneaked up behind him to attach an antipersonnel mine to his belt buckle. "You want some of this?" he cried later, as he climbed into a tank and leveled its huge trunk at my chest. We tittered and played that violent tag until my head ached from the overload. Ethan would never be ready to quit, but he could recognize when he had worn me out, and we would head upstairs again.

By then the family had begun their own virtual war, the talk finally fixed on an ongoing discussion of that unruly dictator, and they would offer up bits of propaganda they had memorized verbatim, or, like a team of assistant coaches, they would hash out the likely strategies of the coming conflict, brandishing smart euphemisms. They spoke as though their words tasted good, and from inside the hyperbaric chamber of Sky Meadow their war must have seemed as easy to orchestrate as a feast. They moved troops, directed infrastructure, anticipated collateral loss, negotiated treaties, purchased allies, formed coalitions, passed bills and resolutions. Without me there to calcify their beliefs, they could explore the gradations that separated each from

the other. Were smart bombs economically efficient? Was it
wise to invade in February? What level of civilian casualty
was acceptable? The teenagers listened and chuckled at the
expectation of sanctioned death.

When I arrived, they would all pause to recalibrate. As a
rule, the family tended to react to me as though I had just
suffered some great loss, or perhaps not too long ago I had
attempted suicide, and a certain delicacy was called for. I was
a person of extreme sensitivity—I couldn't confront the harsh
evils of the world without dissolving into a slithering mess,
and to accommodate me was to provide a kind of nurturance,
to assure themselves they were capable of pity. But if I sat
quietly for a time among them, if I squeezed in on a sofa and
kept to myself, the intersecting lines of debate would begin
again, three or four beams of misinformation. It was the
basic Christian two-step of justifying atrocity in the name
of civilization. It was a celebration of fused, contradictory
platforms. If I stopped listening completely, it would come to
sound like a honeycomb of bees dancing out an accidental
message sure to infect the hive, and I could block it out as
that kind of drone, pleasant in a way, once it lost what was
recognizable in it.

Two days before Christmas found us all in just such a
pose, my post-Halo headache wavering through the song
of the worker bees. The family was ironing out the details
of what to do with the nation-state once they had achieved
victory. "I don't think we're operating with a complete
definition of treachery here," my brother said. The talk
turned to the nature of evil and a precise definition of war.

"State-level belligerents engaged in military action" was met with "organized intergroup violence." "Conflict to control geographical territory" fell to "political terrorism intended to expand sovereign rule." On this note, Ethan launched himself over the arm of the sofa and into my lap. He had been stalking us again. I grunted, and he threw his arm around my neck like a monkey. The family ignored us. "Of course those people want democracy," my mother said. Ethan fingered the back of my neck and looked at my eyes for a moment, measuring me.

And then, quite suddenly, he reached between my legs and grabbed my penis through my pants.

It was so casual a motion that it seemed perfectly normal, really. It lasted only a fraction of a second, and to react to it would have been to appear to have reacted to nothing at all. "Quite frankly, the international community is hardly a community without us," my father said. Ethan smiled and leaned in next to my face. "*I touched your wee-wee!*" he whispered.

I looked about to make sure no one had seen. The buzzing was turning heated. There wasn't anything unusual about Ethan sitting in my lap, and I palmed the boy's spine. "*I know. You shouldn't do that,*" I whispered.

"Why should the Kurds have their own country? Can someone explain that?" my sister said.

"*Why not?*" Ethan said.

"Sure it's about oil," my brother said. "Should it be about something else?"

"*Because it's a private spot.*"

"Realistically, imperialism is the only true solution to world chaos. That's historical fact."

Ethan's lip touched my earlobe. *"Why is it private?"*

My penis had shrunk back against my body, but I could still feel his fingers there. Why was it private? There were reasons. We had descended from a culture that had used a religion based on shame and perverse asceticism as its organizing principle. Our nation, lusty and promiscuous in the media, was in reality repressed on all matters sexual and even physiological. There were reasons, but they weren't really very good reasons, and Ethan wouldn't have understood them anyway. Childhood was made up of suffering in the sense that eventually you figured out the adults were all lying to you. What was there after the scam of Santa? When you were ready to give up fantasy, all there was to replace it was faith, and nobody had answers for the questions that really mattered.

"It's private because that's the rule," I said. *"Do you understand?"*

"I just don't want to go into this thing unless I can see a favorable endgame on the horizon."

Ethan didn't like it, but he nodded. It was the first moment when I had slipped into the role of adult with him. He became sullen.

"Promise," I said. *"Promise you won't touch me there again."*

"Why should we trust the Turks? They got a Muslim government. Elected!"

Ethan sighed. *"Promise,"* he whispered, and he slid off my knee to go play Halo, alone.

✛

Ethan stayed away for a day or so. Christmas came looming
up like a kind of countdown to niceness, that moment when
the conductor would tap his baton and signal for regulated
harmony. The family gathered in the living room. Someone
had hit the remote that ignited the fireplace, and the six-
disc stereo sifted through Johnny Mathis and Bing Crosby.
My brother offered the argument that Christmas trees—the
one that loomed above us was eleven feet tall and filled with
antique ornaments—actually predated Christianity. There
was gathering evidence, he said, that bringing trees into
homes and decorating them began with animist religions.
This received mixed reviews from the family. They exchanged
uncertain looks and touches. It may have all been a trap;
without Ethan there to buoy me, I decided to take it as an
opening and launched into a theory I had been preparing in
my mind. I made some loose segue from Christmas trees to
America (it wasn't hard—the decoration of the tree as a form
of play, capitalism as an expression of game theory—I sort
of fudged the details) and then argued that our nation itself
had become a kind of video game. To be American had long
since come to mean spectating, being a fan of one's country
instead of a team player, investing in domestic interpretation
and spin, inserting faith in a slot that triggered a show that
gave an illusion of control, a vote that may or may not mean
what you thought it did. Didn't we now have colleges for
video games, commercials for them, competitions in them,

didn't we think like video games, export their philosophy, and wage war with the hope that it would resemble them? The republic seemed to think of civilization itself as a kind of video game—take control and blaze the terrain until you run out of lives. To be a superpower meant obtaining an infantilized super-skill, an ultra- or megaweapon, the silly language was all the same, and the only goal was to retain the sanctity of power for as long as possible, because having it meant more lives and a prolonged version of one's society. This brought us back to the unruly dictator—the whole world just then preoccupied with weapons that meant validation. The dictator wanted megapower. He wanted in the game. Didn't we want to destroy him, I said, just to keep him on the sidelines?

The family took all this in silently. It was too much for them. They knew I was crazy, but it was as though I had blasphemed, and you just couldn't chalk that up to insanity.

"Are you even an American?" my father said.

There followed a melee of raw insult. We called a truce almost at once, and in deference to the descending holiday we attempted to establish some common ground, a no-man's-land of morality we could all obey. War is bad, I tried. No, remember the Great War, or the war after that, you couldn't really say they were bad. Evil is a uselessly relative and abstract concept. Hardly, look at the unruly dictator. Killing is wrong. No, they insisted, killing was sometimes the right thing to do.

"Well, that gives you all," I said, "a good deal in common with your average psychopath."

The family looked at the coffee table and held their breath against the noxious air. I couldn't hurt them, or even communicate with them. We all sat for a long moment wondering what family really meant if it was possible to wind up staring at one another across such broad vistas. Then Ethan reappeared. He walked among us quietly. He was wearing my sweater, and the green, I noticed, put a kind of light in his eyes. But the sweater wasn't the reason for his visit.

"Uncle C—, would you come downstairs with me?"

"Not right now, Ethan."

He stared a moment, and I came to understand that it wasn't a usual request; he wished to share some secret with me. He stacked his hands on my knee, and leaned forward.

"*Something happened*," he whispered.

He took my hand as though to lead me to a dance floor. He was entirely intent on our mission. I didn't look back. What would have been the point? The family was relieved, and they spoke of me, I'm sure, in pithy tones of condescending mercy, as though I had just presented with some ghastly symptom of mental illness, some explosive habit that put a strain on all of them, but they could bear that cross if they just stuck together. I didn't hear them speak again.

Ethan's hand fit perfectly inside mine, but his skin was chilled. Something had spooked him. I stopped him on the landing halfway down the stairs.

"Santa already came," he said. "He came *early*."

I hid a smile, thought I understood. Ethan would be receiving dozens of presents that year, and the house was a minefield of stashed toys. The boy had rooted through some closet and turned up something meant for him.

"What did you find?"

"A game," Ethan said. "But I don't understand it."

I was confident. It was whatever program Ethan was to be given in replacement for Halo, and surely I could shepherd him through it. We continued to the television and nuzzled on the sofa. Ethan turned on the game and, while we waited for the program to load, put his head against my arm. But he was still disturbed. He opened his mouth to speak. He paused, and it was perhaps the first time in his life when he would step outside his tiny frame of reference to speak to the larger world.

"I saw Grandpa," he said.

I nodded. "Grandpa's upstairs."

He squared himself so that he could look me in the eye. "No. I saw Grandpa *in the game.*"

For what happened next I offer neither reason nor explanation. The screen twitched and sizzled and blanked, and then called up a fanciful sloping world of perfect streets and pine trees. It was not dread, not exhilaration, but a nameless hybrid of the two that sparked inside me when I recognized it. It was Sky Meadow. The game had begun its story at the base of that apocryphal hill, where the gray-haired guards played gin rummy in their tiny heated hut.

"You see?" Ethan said.

Our view was subjective, and Ethan toggled us toward the gate. The guards popped out, and the boy quickly produced a pistol and shot them both. He stepped around their bodies, then around the hydraulic bollard, which had fooled him the first couple times. It wasn't pretty, he said.

"How . . ." I said.

"I don't know. But wait."

We jogged through the clean landscape, past shrubs so well groomed in reality that their virtual twins rendered them perfectly. Ethan stopped next to a fire hydrant.

"Now watch," he said.

He kicked forward another step, hitting some kind of trigger in the game's programming, and a few yards ahead a little man stepped out from behind a tree. He was unarmed, and took two steps forward before stopping and putting his hands on his hips. It was my father.

"I've come to realize that I just don't enjoy talking to you anymore," the little man said.

Ethan left the controller pad limp in his lap. "That's as far as I've gone."

I asked to see the game's packaging, but it was only a blank container he'd found in a shabby-chic end table. There was no box or manual. The game didn't have a sound track, but every few moments the little version of my father, Ethan's grandpa, shifted his weight and repeated his line.

"I've come to realize that I just don't enjoy talking to you anymore."

Ethan tried to step around Grandpa, but the game wouldn't let him. My father blocked the only path in a labyrinth with one solution. Ethan tried several directions, but we were stuck. Finally I said, "Lieutenant, what weapons do we have?"

There was the pistol he'd used on the guards, a machine gun, and a sniper rifle. "And there's some kind of light-modulating beam weapon," Ethan said.

"Like a laser gun?"

"I guess."

"Use the laser, Ethan," I said. "Use the laser, and blast Grandpa."

Ethan looked back at the screen and shuffled through our armory until the tip of the laser gun aimed out in front of us. He hesitated.

"You do it," the boy said.

He balanced the controller pad on my knee. He squeezed in tighter against my side, splicing our elbows together. I took up the pad and nestled it into my hands, arranging my fingers to the toggles. My father's expression was dense and somewhat annoyed, an expression I probably wear myself on occasion. Only the thought that the game might be some legitimate black magic gave me pause. But then the little man humped again from one leg to the other and began to speak, "I've come to realize—" and I yanked back hard on the trigger.

The weapon glowed an instant before it fired, and its energy shot forward in a sharp beam of pointed bright. It caught my father just above the navel, and two waves quickly spread over him—the first a shine as the power of the weapon began to destroy him, and then a hole, an expanding void as the beam took him apart, shuttling him off disassembled to some awful dimension. He was half gone before he had time to react, this by lifting his hand to watch it precede him into purgatory. Then he was gone and all was still.

We listened for a shriek from above, but the real Sky
Meadow was as quiet as its tiny counterpart. It was just a
game. Residual power from the laser flicked once in the air
where Grandpa had stood, and then the path was clear.

"Keep going," Ethan said.

The game led to my parents' house, a maze within the
maze, and once there we were confronted with versions
of the entire family, all delivering some accusation before
I vaporized them. "Admit it, you think people who have
children are just wasting their time," my choppy mother
said. I hit her as she dived behind the dining table. My sister
popped out of a bathroom, compact in hand. "Sometimes,
C—, even your vocabulary, it's like you're saying you're
better than us." The light modulator turned her inside
out. "Quite frankly," Ethan's father said, "liberals are the
brainwashed masses of the Cult of the Academy." I got
him with a head shot, and Ethan didn't even flinch. When
Grandpa reappeared—"I'm Christian like the next man,
but . . ."—I realized it wasn't murder, even in the game. The
family kept reappearing. They were a multiplying immortal
army of horrifying rhetoric. "Of course I vote my checkbook—
isn't that what you're *supposed* to do?" "They buy our movies.
We *gave* them television. They should love us." "Capitalism
is all about competition, and war is the purest expression of
economics—or whatever." I ticked them off as they appeared,
but soon they were coming too quickly; the game had an
automatic difficulty adjustment, and it was learning from
my pattern of fire. The family was all on-screen at once,
multiclones burbling rubbish, and when I could no longer

hold them back I turned and ran us down the stairs, to the guest quarters, to where Ethan and I then sat, and when the game pulled up the room, there we were, two heads on the sofa watching a screen inside the screen, and another screen, and an infinity there too tiny to see.

Ethan climbed up on his knees to look behind us, but of course there was nothing there. Back on the television, my double climbed from the sofa and announced, "We inhabit a postclassic failing democracy!"

I stopped to consider a version of mortality. Would the act of annihilating myself amount to murder or suicide, would it be wrong or noble? Ethan swiveled back to await my decision. He was poker-faced about it, and I realized that our affection would never be greater than this, that it was based in megabits of RAM and high-def pixilation, and that our version of compassion was best understood in those terms, in that information. My time with Ethan was an affair, and it would end as affairs ended. I would look back on a pleasure initially so complete that it would seem virtual in remembrance, an impossible fiction. We had arrived for this instant at an identical plane of concern and desire, but we had descended to that spot from opposite poles, and soon enough we would be yanked back to separate realities like puppets on puppet strings.

I fired, and because we were still pressed together, the laser treated us as one.

From there, the game became more familiar. Our invasion had tripped my mother's alarm system, and as once had happened so long ago, law enforcement personnel descended on the house. FBI burst through the doors, SWAT rappelled down the walls, all of them armed and anxious to deliver justice. They were the bad guys, but Ethan didn't seem to notice. "My turn, Uncle C—," he said, and he snatched the controller pad away to enter the fray.

Christmas arrived on time and the predictable civility came about quite naturally. We acted out the script of the morning, exchanges that gave the family a warm sensation of ritual and custom, as though we were a company reunited to act out an old play. Familiar lines came spiced with tradition. We traded books we thought the others should read, clothes we thought the others should wear. We warmed in the heat of the artificial fire and sang a birthday ditty to Baby Jesus. Ethan tore through his pirate's treasure of gifts. There was pot roast for dinner. "I'll take the cooked part," I told my father, as he sliced the rare beast and passed the slabs around.

The peace held until I left, and I distributed hugs and farewells across my packed bag as a taxi sat in the drive burping clumps of fume. It had snowed Christmas Eve, an idyllic storm laying a comforter across the northeast. Ethan managed only the briefest of good-byes at my departure—an embrace of consolation, the hug one gives a stranger when a moment nevertheless calls for affection. Our real good-bye had come some time before. The family had shuttled Ethan off to bed early on Christmas Eve, far too early for him, really. It gave the rest of us time to finish our wrapping,

and position the presents for that year's photograph, and
sip our eggnog and brandy, and hold that kind of holiday
court that is possible when the world is at peace. My father
engaged the alarm system when the lights of the Christmas
tree lulled us with their foggy sheen. He turned off the fire.
We all retired to our quarters. Mine for the week had been
my father's study, furnished with a large contoured globe at
perfect scale and a tattered old leather armchair that was
the third piece of furniture my parents had ever owned. My
father's sculpted bust sat on the desk and watched me climb
into a bed like a cot in a makeshift ward. Out the window, Sky
Meadow knew nothing of the holiday except for a street lamp
near the house that had burned out, a malfunction that would
have been repaired at once if anyone had been on duty. The
community took on an inky brand of black.

I wasn't quite asleep, but was already dreaming of my
beautiful lady friend, when Ethan's knock on the door
entered my fantasy as her touch on my cheek. The boy crept
into the room and sat on the bed. He had detached his video
device from the television downstairs and brought it with
him. He had the new game as well.

"Can't sleep. Want to play?" he said.

We tiptoed out of the room. We moved forward a few steps
through the dark before Ethan stopped and held me back.
He pointed down to one of the infrared beam boxes shooting
its invisible motion sensor across the floor. He indicated the
angle it took. That's what he had been doing all the while
he had hunted us in the living room. He knew where all the
trip wires were. He straddled the light, and I followed his

high-stepping lead through the musty museum. He stopped at the Christmas tree, the presents he would raze come morning, and bulged his eyes—the night's ghost had already come and gone. It wasn't that Ethan still believed in Santa Claus. It was that he resisted disbelieving, and that might have been the only good definition of innocence left. We were a nation with an alarm system. The family believed it was too pretty to die. In the face of all that, what could you say to anyone to address good and bad, right and wrong?

Ethan connected the game to the television in the kitchen. He sat in my lap and left the volume low. It all started as it had before, the gatehouse and the guards and the hydraulic bollard, but it began to change as soon as we jogged into its perfect light. Sky Meadow morphed to an alien forest, my family to the troops of some hostile regime. It was similar to what we had seen the day before, but different enough so that it seemed possible that Ethan and I had simply made a mistake in observing it. The boy weighed against me, warm and twitching as he played. I touched his heavy head. It's natural enough to question the validity of daylight from the stupor of a dreamy night, and love for my nephew seemed inevitable just then.

AUTOPOIESIS FOR THE COMMON MAN

I was dating two nurses at once. They were both older than
me by a good margin. All they had in common with each
other was nursehood and microbiology. But really there was
very little difference between us. All autopoietic beings, after
all, chemically maintain their identities despite constant
environmental perturbation. Joan and Marci taught me that
trees and people have common eukaryotic roots—we share
mitochondria, Golgi bodies, and sperm tails—and that the
ultimate ancestor is a DNA-containing microbial cell. The
genome trapped within the plasma membrane of eukaryotes
is an entity capable of indeterminate growth. It is immortal.
Which is not to say it is flawless. Indeed, to err is more than
human, it is biological.

Joan was wiry and charmingly goofy. She lived in a trailer
park. Her hair was long and red, frayed like antique textile,
sexy *because* it looked old. She almost never wore underwear,
only tattered bras or briefs when she did, and she played
bass guitar in a band of failed minstrels. She once plucked
out a song for me in her nightie, bobbing her hairy head and
biting her lip as she strummed. She was forty.

Marci was the ex-wife of a university law professor,
and lived on a hill in a Victorian with a dozen rooms and a

semicircular driveway. She was pretty and petite, cropped hair dyed a sleek black, but for all the time I knew her she had a blemish on her cheek, a wart that said all she herself would not about what it was like to have your husband leave you for a student. Marci kept busy in community cleanup groups, had three darling sons, and was proud of her kitchen. She was forty-two.

Joan was a home health aid. She darted through town in a clunker, a bag of syringes on the seat next to her, and gave injections to people who needed them but couldn't do it themselves. She made more as an LPN, she said, than she had as a secretary. The injections, which were generally painful, were gratifying to her because she didn't like most of her patients.

Marci was a full RN, but only volunteered at the local hospice, caring for terminally ill children who arrived one month and invariably died by the next. At first, she said, you cry for them. You cry for every damn one. But before long, there's one you don't cry for, either because he's not there that long, or because you know he's better off dead. That clears the way. Pretty soon you're not crying for any of them.

✛

Back then I told people I was a writer, but in secret I was working at a hardware store. I made enough to pay the rent and the heat, and occasionally had time to scribble out stories I never liked when they were finished. Sometimes, after our shift, my friend and coworker suggested we stop at a nearby beer garden. It was here that I met Joan, at an old warped picnic table littered with plastic beer pitchers. In retrospect, it makes sense as the brewing of beer is fundamentally the autopoiesis of brewer's yeast under warm, wet conditions.

Joan sat alone with a book. My friend and coworker knew her, or had known her, but he had a girlfriend his own age by then. He introduced us.

"This is Joan," he said. "She has no life, and you have no life. Maybe together you can make life."

He wandered off into the garden's oblivion, and Joan and I stared at each other. I looked at her book. It was called *The Conjugal Cyst*. Microbiology, I gathered, and eventually I learned that it was the text for a course Joan was taking as part of a continuing education program.

A water treatment plant loomed over the garden. Its odor surfed the breeze toward us across a fetid alley, and provided the context for my only relevant factoid. I nodded at the book.

"The purification of sewage is the autopoietic activity of methane-producing bacteria," I said.

"How sexy that you know that," Joan said.

The next moment might have been awkward, but she continued with a lecture.

"The cell is the minimal unit of both autopoiesis and reproduction," she said. "Lederberg proved definitively that bacteria have a sex life: a donor passes DNA to a recipient. It's like nursing. Genetic recombination began as an enormous health delivery system." She went on to explain that even the simplest bacterial sex was not at all simple, and that from a cellular vantage point human sex was identical to that of protistan microbes. She pushed together two beer puddles on the surface of our table to form a sample colony of microbial orgy, then explained that sex had come about as a response to threats in the environment, primarily ultraviolet light. "Dinomastigotes form non-fertilizing conjugal cysts to help one another survive cold spells. Isn't it romantic?"

I agreed that it was.

The sound of a band drifted down on us from a window, a rocking angry sentiment. As one pissed-off song ended we heard laughter, tingly laughter, and at the end of it a woman called happily, "Oh, fuck!"

Joan passed a finger slowly through the moisture of her beer puddle. "Mitosis and meiotic sex arose as the organizing phenomena from the mire and confusion of microbial community life. Bacteria often engage in sex without reproduction. Sometimes it's lethal, producing no offspring and destroying both partners. They do it anyway."

She put the wet finger in her mouth. I had nothing to say.

"It's with protoctists that meiotic-fertilization cycles evolved. Fungi hold the record for biotic potential, but some bacteria reproduce three times per hour. That's me flirting, just so you know."

"I know," I said.

Joan wet her finger again, but this time used the moisture to spell out a message on the table. She wrote it upside down so it read from my side.

I want you bad.

I used my own finger to continue the message. It still read from my side.

I want you badly.

She rested her chin on her fist, smiling. "Grammar is such a turn-on," she said.

We said good-bye to my friend and coworker and went to the little house I rented, my dark den with some land and shade trees. We took turns reading passages from *The Conjugal Cyst* as though it were a manual of love. Outcrossing, Joan narrated, was the mating of two organisms that were no more closely related to one another than to other members of the general population. We laughed and hugged, and then we used our bodies to form a tight cyst that protected us against the dark. Joan left late that night, and I stood by the door until the taillights of her clunker wavered around the bend. She was back the next day at high noon.

"My DNA needs mending," she said.

She climbed into my house and then into my arms. She had forgotten her book the night before, and I had spent most of the morning reading it.

"I should have told you this before," I said. "I have herpes. Type I. Genital."

"Oh, I've had that for years. Anyway, the transfer of a virus from host to recipient is just another form of chromosomal sexuality." She took a step back and pulled off her shirt. "I've been driving around all morning sticking people with needles. Now, it's my turn."

Later, when we lay on my bed, exhausted, Joan took a deep breath and then spoke: "Sex has its analogies. If a village grows to double its original size, that's mitosis. If the village then splits into two villages through colonization, that's meiosis. The donor's DNA must align with the recipient's DNA accurately enough so that the recombination event does not create inversions, disjunctions. There's danger for both. Sex is the joining of genetic material from two sources in a single individual, but does not require an increase in the total number of individuals. In fact, the number may decrease."

She ran a hand over my chest, her fingers playing my little hairs as though they were the strings of her guitar.

"Lord, I hope I don't have to kill myself over you," she said.

✪

Marci I met at a bookstore poetry reading. I went to poetry readings, I admit, to make sure the poets weren't up to anything interesting. Before the poet, whoever he was, took the stage, I flipped through a coffee table book on cooking. I was considering taking up cooking. I had the idea it would improve things.

"Oh, do you cook?" Marci said. She was beside me, pert and ready.

I looked at her, and thought to impress her with a tidbit from *The Conjugal Cyst*. "Sexual dimorphism is the visible difference between potential gamont partners."

Marci's education was more complete than Joan's, and she didn't hesitate. "There are at least as many mechanisms of mate recognition as there are species of organism," she said. "Probably many more."

We gaped at one another, but the poet began before we could continue. I looked at Marci's wart through the first few poems. It was red and ugly, a virus in and of itself, but she was still quite pretty.

I asked her to coffee when the poet was done and the applause had faded, at the moment when, had I not said anything, we would have floated away from each other into the street's vast soup of amoebae and diatoms. We discussed the reading. Marci liked it, I found things to say. I told her I was a writer, and I was careful to speak in complete sentences. As a kind of punctuation to the conversation, I traced my finger along the rim of my coffee cup. Marci told me stories of the hospice children she cared for, but watched my finger as she spoke, and I knew it was this that made the difference for her, that tipped the scale in my favor.

"The exact extent of bacterial conjugation is unknown," she said, once we knew one another, roughly. "Some species mate with enough consistency, however, that they can be studied in a lab."

"Maybe they like to be watched."

"But the mating is always polarized. The donor always grabs 'his' mate and forces his genes into 'her.' It's never reciprocal."

"Never?" I said.

She smiled, and we split the bill. She gave me a business card with just her name and address on it: MARCI REED, 132 E. WINDSWIFT LANE. Reed was her married name, retained because it was the name of her children and that made a difference. Her divorce was not yet final.

"I want you to put my clitoris in your mouth," she said, our first time together. "I know you're young, but how can you not have done this before?"

"Teach me," I said.

She thought a moment. "The eukaryotic cell wraps and moves discrete parts of itself—it has a predilection to engulfing things. Originally, protists cannibalized one another without digestion, doubling their chromosomes without fertilization."

I gave it a shot.

"Ah, there ya go," Marci said.

After a time, she climbed on top of me and began to move. *The Conjugal Cyst* said that non-mitotic cells, no matter how elegant their motility, tended to die. It made me sad. Marci called my penis the "little undulipodia" after the long waving organelles that allowed for movement in eukaryotes. Undulipodia were once free-living bacterial entities. Marci detailed the theory of their development as she twisted and plunged on top of me.

"They were *pounded* down from symbionts to structures *inside* the cell," she said, gasping. "The extent of the *merger* was unprecedented in *intimacy*."

I had to exit early as we didn't have a condom between us. But Marci grabbed onto the little undulipodia, and it was nice, pulsing into her hand. She rolled beside me and examined the goop.

"Sperm contains 3,300 micrograms of DNA. It's very efficient, but *Gymnodinium nelsoni* contains 143,000 micrograms."

"I'm only human," I said.

"Now what do I do with this?"

"Wipe it on my back. I'm taking a shower anyway."

"I never did this before," she said, and smeared the stuff across my shoulders, the back of my neck, and my buttocks.

✛

I met Joan and Marci in the summer, but by autumn things were very different.

Joan became convinced that I did not wish to be seen in public with her. It was only partly true. Several times we had eaten together at a supermarket restaurant counter, I reminded her, and we had taken a number of long walks together in a park that was a public place, I argued, even if no one else was there. By mid-September, she had begun dating another man who agreed to go to bars with her, but only on weekends. I left phone messages for her—to return her book—but she never answered them.

Marci I pushed away on my own. She had tried on me that forceful bacterial-style love, bringing her boys over for unexpected visits, sending me notes in the mail full of painstaking script, and arriving unannounced late one night for sex, which struck me as exciting at first, then frightening, and finally exciting again. At the equinox, I told her I was not ready for the life she lived and nor did I deserve it. We embraced, she told me she loved me, and I thanked her for the sentiment. A week later she flew to Seattle to visit a man she had met at a hospice staff reunion a month earlier. She came home engaged.

✛

Autopoiesis, *The Conjugal Cyst* explained, came from the Greek for "self-making," but in modern scientific usage it was more closely aligned with "self-maintenance." Only in certain phyletic lineages had sex come to be required in both autopoiesis and reproduction. The fact that human beings evolved from one of these lineages has created an unrealistic view of biological sexuality. In fact, it isn't at all clear why autopoietic entities are divided into individuals that reproduce; it simply seems to be the case. Men and women are not different from one another because sexual species are better equipped to confront a dynamic environment, but because of a set of historical accidents that permitted the survival of ancestral protists.

Even today, bacterial cells exposed to intense ultraviolet light undergo lysis—they explode. In early October of that year there came a day when I felt bloated and infected and desirous. A phage burst was imminent. Meiotic-fertilization cycles are closely related to environmental cycles, and as fall colors swept across our town my alchemy was stirred as though in response to a threat. The word *male* means an organism that produces small gametes that swarm, but the term may also be applied to one of the gametes. Male sex cells are so designated because of their propensity to move, and a large motile gamete is called an ookinete. That October day, I became an ookinete. I called my friend and coworker, but his protective cyst was already complete. I was alone and exposed. Before I knew it I found myself wandering through the year's first chill, driving the town, already drunk, missing gears and slurring the words I spoke aloud to myself. My quest was for a like other, one without an F-factor but equipped with a surface substance attractive to one with an F-factor. She would be a conspirator of similar need, she would long to be new in the sexual sense. Why she would want this I didn't know. I was simpler. I was a vulnerable exhabitant. I longed to borrow undamaged DNA, and donate my own. I felt totipotent. I needed to outcross.

It was still early when I found myself exhausted from the search, shrouded over a beer mug at one moment full and crisply cold, the next warm and empty as my soul. Before me was football on a TV screen, men in tight pants contorting and swarming, ookinetes staring hard at one another while yet more ookinetes stared hard at them. For a time, I felt I understood the game well enough to play.

The female anchor of the halftime news update, rattling statistics of the day's homicides in the nearby metropolis, proved the vision to slap me from ugly stupor. She recalled Marci's chirpy tone and clipped hair with a macabre sentence or two. I ran through Marci's mole pattern in my mind—I had it memorized, and connected the dots over her back and belly to mythical shapes. Her joint structure, I remembered, had excited me beyond the usual call of joints, and her neck, I had once thought, was the secret destination of all ookinetes. I reconsidered having set Marci aside, regardless of how wise and mature a decision it had seemed at the time. In the span of a minute or two, I played out a life with her, moving through it at super-warp, granting benefit to all doubt and slowing only for scenes of our fused mixis. I found it all nutrient-rich and agreeable. One life was surely as viable an option as another, I thought, and to refuse them all, as I had until then, was a kind of doom. A man who is infertile is autopoietic but unable to reproduce, *The Conjugal Cyst* had warned. He has forfeited genetic continuity. In an evolutionary sense, he is already dead.

I dialed Marci's number into the first phone I could find. Again, I was careful with my sentences.

"Is this a mating call?" Marci said.

"Sort of."

"You know, you don't really see stylized mating behavior until the higher vertebrates."

"I'm a mammal," I said.

She agreed to see me, but asked for twenty minutes of lag. I stopped at a convenience store for coffee, and chewed an entire pack of gum.

When I arrived we hugged liked dear friends brought together for a sad occasion. She had tea ready in a porcelain pot. We sat together on a fat flowered sofa, reflections of casual friendliness, organelles draped here and there to suggest what was possible between us. I asked after her new fiancé. She pressed her lips and said he was a good egg, and after all I had learned I wondered what she meant by it.

After an interval I felt fair, I told her what I had come to tell her, that I had reconsidered our break, that her life, which had first struck me as overwhelmingly contained, now seemed like the essence of hope in a world gone mad with hate and death. I told her I missed her children and reminded her that she had described their taking to me as miraculous. (In fact, I thought the boys had been largely deferential.) Love was the important thing now, I said, the love of coworkers, of partners, of perfect pairs bound to one another by the powerful twine of a collective heart. Marci stared at a spot before her as I spoke, thinking of our possible life, a life she had already imagined a season before and surely much more slowly. I was convincing as I believed all that I said, believed, in fact, in every sentimental vision I had ever known, the sappy equations of oneness metaphoric and endosymbiotic. At last, I fell silent and leaned forward to await her decision.

"I have to know!" she said, sliding across the cushions. "I'm just—I'm sorry, but I have to know!"

We embraced and kissed and lived a moment that would be unblanched by subsequent imaginings. I felt the tip of my nose brush her wart—still prominent, but healing nicely.

We moved to her bedroom and undressed, kissing and touching, stroking and grabbing each other with tender strength. We ducked beneath the sheets of her massive bed, thrashing off the coolness. Marci climbed on top of me, pinned my shoulders, and forced a moment of stillness.

"I'm married to one man, engaged to another, and here I am with you," she said.

"It's exponential cheating," I said, and she laughed at a vision of herself thought impossible until now.

We brought our tongues together, cilia threaded in the airtight cyst of our mingled mouths. It seemed to me that the proximity of brains made this the most intimate of couplings.

We were locked together for some time when there came a minute knocking on the bedroom door, softer than the scratch of a cat.

"Oh! Get up, get up!" Marci whispered. "Go over—get over there!"

She pushed me, naked, into a low-ceilinged nook of the room, an angular recess that in daylight was a charming imperfection to the impressive old home. Marci answered the door, and of course it was her youngest, Colin, awakened by thirst or a dream. The boy had turned on a lamp in the hall, but the light failed to reach my little cave. I stood hunched like a troll.

Marci kneeled and spoke quietly to the boy, shaping breathy promises of love. She looked over her shoulder at me once, and moved to block her son's line of sight. As they spoke I took stock of my cranny, noticing for the first time in a number of visits to the room a framed picture hung low on the wall. It was a pencil portrait, and I was stunned when I studied it and recognized the face. It was Marci as a much younger woman, a fresh-faced ingenue just two or three years younger than my age of the moment. Her hair was long, her face tight and flattered by the artist, her expression a joy that I had never yet seen her deploy. The wart on her cheek was gone. Or, rather, yet to emerge.

Marci sent Colin off with a hug and a kiss, a pat on his head and one for his stuffed bear. She shut the door again. The room went black, and after a moment the night flushed in through the panes. We stood opposed in the blue light, and Marci looked at me strangely.

"Seeing you there," she said. "Seeing you there crouched and hiding."

"You pushed me there," I said.

"I know." She touched her index finger to the divot of her upper lip. "Many organisms have given up mixis while retaining meiosis. Many, especially gram-positive bacteria, do not engage in sex at all."

"It's because their cell walls are too thick," I said.

"Correct. But the trend in dense, educated regions of the world is toward a decrease in the frequency of mixis."

"Not all sexual events require fusion," I tried.

"You're not ready for this." She tipped her head, and made a self-congratulatory gesture to the room and its furnishings. "A bacterial donor that offers too many of its genes dies."

"I think I am ready."

"No. You were right before. I have a lot of love, but you're not ready for it yet."

I breathed a moment, then sat on the edge of the bed and arranged my clothes. I was humiliated, but it would last only as long as I was in the presence of her victory. Marci sat next to me and corrected my socks, laying them in easy reach as I stuffed my shirt into my pants.

She reached to cup my cheek. "You're a dear boy. I'll always think that."

"You're crazy," I said, and I grabbed my socks and found the door in the dark.

✚

Human sexual pleasure has more to do with reproduction than with sex. In the earliest animals, reproduction became trapped within sexuality. There were many attempts to escape, but it never disappeared completely. Sexual systems that appear similar may in fact have evolved independently. I reminded myself of this as I drove to Joan's. Joan was the same genus as Marci, but she was of a different species. She was the one woman who would understand my need. Fantasies were unnecessary; I had only to appeal to her own vicious requirements. She could ignore my messages, but she had never denied my actual self.

It was a weeknight. The trailer park was dark. The houses themselves, a cluster of dark shanties, squatted out there like a moribund herd of bison, each waiting for the next tornado that would funnel in and snatch them to the sky. The walls of the homes had rusted to a faded orange, and the windows were still plasticked from the last brutal winter. People had put out their plants to catch the morning dew, their cats to do nocturnal battle with an army of shit-eating rats. There were cars on cinder blocks, wandering children who belonged to no one, and from everywhere the soft voice of television as companion and lullaby.

I moved along the dark dirt road, creeping on my snow tires. Joan's trailer looked abandoned. However, her clunker sat parked beside the propane tanks, oxidizing. I turned off my lights and drifted in, careful though I intended to wake her anyway. I sat a moment behind the wheel.

The door, a sandwich of plywood and cardboard, stood open but for her chain lock. I could see a slice of her living room, her couch with crumpled afghans, her shiny guitar standing upright against an amplifier. I had to pull the door shut to knock on it properly.

She didn't answer. The door was soggy, and knocking any harder meant risking its integrity. I opened it again and put my lips to the crack.

"Joan! Joan-baby!" I let my voice gradually become louder. "Joan! Joan!"

A light came from the bedroom, and the sleepy footfalls that approached caused the whole house to wobble slightly. Joan opened the door without looking to see who it was.

"Are you alone?" I said.

"Just one time," she said, rubbing her eyes. She looked at me finally. "Oh, hello. Well, come in."

She wore a veil-thin nightgown. The light from the bedroom pushed through it and showed her body as in X-ray. She was barefoot, and stepped lightly on her pads toward the kitchen.

"Want a beer?"

"Desperately."

"I'm going to smoke weed. You don't, do you? Why is that?"

"My upbringing."

"You don't mind if I?"

"No."

She brought to the sofa two cans of a cheap domestic and her pot paraphernalia. Joan didn't smoke tobacco, and looked unpracticed preparing her little spark plug pipe. When she took her first hit her face dissolved to culinary ecstasy.

"I'm glad you're here," she said. "There's something I have to tell you."

I opened my beer, gargled and swallowed. I took Joan's feet into my lap and warmed them with my hands.

"From a philosophical-evolutionary point of view," she said, "sex, rescue from death, cannibalism, and lack of digestion all started out as pretty much the same thing. Agreed?"

"Okay," I said, only half-listening. I ran my palm up her leg, past her knee to where it became substantial, formidable in its musculature.

"However, if meiosis is to evolve, a stable mitotic division cycle is a must."

I stopped. "What are you getting at?"

She held up a finger. "The production of a human infant is primarily a form of mitotic expansion. The assumption that hostile environments maintain sexuality is intuitively appealing but ultimately unjustifiable."

"What did you do?" I said.

She breathed and looked at me. "I had an abortion. Just the other day. It may have been yours."

I reached to touch her face, run my thumb through the cavity under her cheekbone. "It's okay. Sex in most organisms is still divorced from reproduction."

"That's why I haven't called. My fifth."

"Fifth?"

"There were four others. One more for the even half dozen."

"That and the Bermuda trip," I said.

"Yeah, right. Ha."

She watched me move toward her, and I kissed her first on her cheek, then on her mouth. I could taste the beer and the pot, and I thought of the way that the taste of a person's mouth becomes another means of recalling them after it's all over.

"I love your hair," I said, raking my fingers through it. "Have I told you that?"

"Yes," she said. "I think so. My hair. I don't know."

"Like flagella. Long and few per cell. Like a witch."

"A witch. That I haven't heard. Ha-ha."

I peeled the afghans off the couch, moving forward as there was room. I found her underneath it all and slipped my hands beneath her rib cage, holding her like a wicker basket. I kissed her ear, and heard her open her mouth to breathe. I listened for the sweet vocals sure to come, but instead she pushed me back and locked her elbows to hold me there, a forearm away.

"Listen, honey," she said. "I would. I probably would. But I can't. It's too soon."

"A sexual event," I said, "requires only one parent to be an autopoietic entity."

She turned her head. "Do you know what they do? Up there?"

I gently reached between her legs. "If you want, I'll kiss it and make it better."

"No." She shook her head and pushed me out to the full length of her arms. "That's it. You're leaving, okay? You're going."

I stayed where I was. She was motionless, looking down between us, waiting for me to obey. I stood up.

"Are you okay to drive?" Joan said. "Because I'm not."

"I'll get there. It's fine."

"Good. Do you understand everything that I said?"

"I think so."

"Because I had to tell you. Even if it's after." She walked me to the door, a palm at my back. "Well, okay then. Take care and drive safe. Call me sometime."

She locked the chain behind me.

Because it resembles the process of mutation, sex has long been assumed to be a major factor in the generation of evolutionary novelty. But it's as much a sink as a source—variety produced by sex is simply nullified by further sex. Yet all eukaryotes—compact populations of cells in the form of cats, penguins, rosebushes, slime molds, and people—pine for meiosis-fertilization ridiculously.

I came out from the trailer park and drifted through the barren pond of our town. I was drunk and purposeless again, and as soon as I saw the neon light of a tavern I realized that neon lights are signals for those already drunk and wandering. They are beacons for ookinetes.

The front room of the bar was empty, but the back room was alive with music and smoke and the smack of pool balls. I climbed a stool and dug into my pocket for cash.

A hand caught my wrist. The fingers were warm, and I felt a nail graze my skin.

"Wait, I'll buy you one."

She was chubby and pretty and young. She straddled the stool next to me, eyes wandering. The barman brought us beer.

"My name's Cristina," she said. "My friends are in the back. They're playing pool. I don't play pool."

"It's a stupid game," I said. "It's dillydallying and physics and symbolism."

"Exactly. That's why I don't play."

"How long have you been here?"

"All night. I have a test in the morning."

"You're a student?"

"Nursing," she said.

I swiveled on my stool to face her. Our four knees touched. I said, "The zygospore of black bread molds is produced by an orgy of fertilizing nuclei."

"Wow," Cristina said.

"That's me flirting," I said, "just so you know."

She gave a drunken laugh, rolling her eyes and running her tongue over her teeth, trying on her sexiness. She reached to touch my thigh, perhaps to see if I was real.

"Listen," I said. "I'm going to go home. It's been a long night for me. But let me drive you. You have a test."

"That's actually a good idea," Cristina said. She started to rise, then sat upright in her chair for an announcement. "Outcrossing has never been shown to confer a definite evolutionary advantage."

"True," I said. "But it reduces the chances of deleterious alleles."

She squinted at me and laughed.

It took us a moment to find my car in the dark. She told me where she lived. I drove us to the end of the street and hesitated there.

I pointed to the right. "It's that way to your dorm, but it's the other way to my house. Which way should I turn?"

Cristina looked off to the right and then to the left, into our various possible futures together. The night was hitting her hard now, and her head lolled a circle on her neck like a top near to falling. She looked out my windshield, splattered with dirt and mud and bugjuice, an ugly mural that was a record of my night, my trips here and there, all the hope and bad news. Through the first three billion years of evolutionary time, *The Conjugal Cyst* had said, sex was not required for autopoiesis, growth, or reproduction. Now, it is possible to imagine a future in which mixis itself has become superfluous, a time in which evolution will limit the central nervous system feedback needed to produce the pleasure that leads to reproduction. Sex may be a billion-year blip. But this was the furthest thing from Cristina's mind at the moment, and finally she pointed straight ahead, through the intersection where we were stopped, toward a row of trees and the stones of a graveyard just beyond. Her eyes closed, consciousness wavering as her decision was made.

"Keep going," she said, and she passed out beside me.

MANIKIN

Not until later did they notice the items missing through the house, a quick dip of stuff more suggestive of an anthropologist than a thief: a baseball glove, a plate, one of a set of four figurines, a photo, a pen holder, a piece of jewelry. Specimens. All collected in a pillowcase that was also missing—this was how they pieced it together—and the perpetrator, one of their own, made off in the night for who really knew where.

Van came downstairs that morning and found his mother, Brenda, seated at the kitchen table. Brenda sat limp in her chair as though stunned from her night's rest, but really she was caught in recoil at the contents of a brief note that had been left behind, the proof of the crime.

Brenda, Gone to Tulsa. Brad.

The note was pinned to the table with a salt shaker. The message had an odd rhythm to it, Van thought, like the notes of a descending scale. At fifteen, Van knew musical order when he heard it. Brad was his father. Had been his father. Already the tense was confusing. But while Brenda soaked in the pain of it, Van found the news easier to reconcile, and he took comfort in the thought that he would now join the ranks of children-of-broken-homes at school; they got more

attention and better grades, and from a distance the bond
between them seemed strong and incalculably deep.

Van sat next to Brenda. He had never before thought
of her by her given name. She seemed quite young to
him then—she was thirty-six—and he saw at once in her
new station what she herself could not: the potential for
something better than what she had managed thus far. A
single square of sunlight from the window over the sink cut
them both in half, warming Brenda's left side and Van's right.

"Tulsa," Brenda said, "is 'a slut' spelled backward."

Van didn't say anything, first to determine whether she
was correct, then to interpret it. She was suggesting Brad
had left her for another woman, which was probably true. It
was dismissal in the form of humorous quip, but it was a joke
meant to convey fury with hyperbole.

They were silent until Kara arrived.

Kara, seventeen, tossed her hair as she read the note.
The glowing strands dripped away from her fingers as she
comprehended it, and Van couldn't help noticing it was sexy,
that motion, and that it was designed that way. His sister was
a sexy girl, but it wouldn't last her long or get her far.

"I'm not surprised," Kara said, sitting down. "Are you
surprised?"

She meant either of them, Kara needing someone to speak
at such a moment, needing discourse to fetter her angst.
But neither Van nor Brenda spoke, and Kara stared at the
tabletop. She was a popular girl, and Van could see that her
first reaction, similar to his, was to weigh what effect this
development would have on her relationships at school. Brad

had not been a mean father. But nor had he compared to the loving patrons of television, the polite dads of Van's friends. He had approached the role, Van thought, as though it were a commercial spot. A bad poet would have said he loved with half a heart.

Kara picked up the salt shaker, the note's paperweight, and turned it as though it were a relic. Then she said, "Where's the pepper?"

It was gone. They began to notice the other items missing as well: a knife, an alarm clock, a canister of tennis balls, a stuffed animal, a telephone. They called to one another through the house to catalog the damages, but it was unclear whether they were performing simple stock work or attempting to diagnose the thief. The items Brad had left behind made a list as potentially revealing: photo albums, his dog, Christmas ornaments, three hundred dollars, a .22 bolt-action target rifle. They returned to the kitchen once the inventory was complete.

"I should call the cops right now," Brenda said.

Her reaction was more interesting as twisted linguistics, Van thought.

"What for?" Kara said. "It's *his* stuff. Useless junk."

"He's crazy," Brenda said. "Walking off with a bunch of random crap."

The house, Van thought, sported a new and conspicuous quality of lightness. "It's not random," he said. "There's order. There's pattern."

Brenda gave a masculine guffaw. "You'll have to explain that one to me, Dr. Metaphysics."

There weren't any words that wouldn't aggravate her further. "It's like this," Van said, and with his finger he traced a circle on the table.

✪

Over the next several days Van noticed heightened awareness in himself, increased emotional efficiency. He *felt* better, and knew that he felt better. It hit him like a virus. Brenda and Kara were infected as well, but they were too steeped in bitterness to notice. All three of them had been caught off guard by the theft and departure, and as though to avoid another shock they had assumed a mode of lingering crisis. It made them more calculating if more cold, more intense if less pleasant, more intelligent if not happy. Van had insight into Brad's spree: the items he had lifted were all easily replaced, the holes filling in quickly like sand filling a hole at the beach. It was part of the message.

The oddest behavior came from Brad's dog, Charlie, a rottweiler. Charlie seemed genuinely afraid to nudge any of the remaining masters for food. The dog drank from the toilets for three days until Brenda took to filling its bowl.

At school, Van's teachers, as he had predicted, paid closer attention to him once word came down that Brad had abandoned them. Kara parlayed the news to a center stage moment among her friends, and one day after school Van's English teacher, Mr. Finger, called out to him near the buses and pulled him aside. Mr. Finger was young, twenty-eight, and Van knew for a fact that he had briefly dated the

divorced mothers of two other students. Mr. Finger said that
he had heard about Van's family's difficulties, and asked if
Van had ever kept a journal.

"No," Van said.

"Well, you should," Mr. Finger said. "And you should write
about *this*."

Van had no idea at all why he should write something
down when there would be no one to read it. By the
time Mr. Finger was done talking, Van's bus had squealed
away from the school. The walk home was two miles with
shortcuts through two fenced yards and a small park. These
neighborhoods looked liked paintings, Van thought as he
passed through them, but not good ones. Clouds shifting
in the near distance, high hills that gave a sense of secure
walls, perfect homes and clean curbs and upright mailboxes
with flags raised for urgent dispatches. It was hollow art. He
imagined himself posed in such a work, a kid trudging along
with no books, no fishing pole, no lunch box, basketball, radio,
or sidekick. Where, in such a painting, he thought, would
such a boy be going?

"Hey!"

Van was in the park now, and the voice was hollered but
far off yet. A man stood over near the swing sets, alone, much
like a figure in a painting himself.

"Hey!" the man called again, and now his arm beckoned
Van along with a huge curling motion.

Van started the walk over. The man put his hands in his
pockets and kicked at the sandbox sand as he waited. The
man wore a thick brown beard over most of his face. The rest

of his hair was long and wavy. He gave a hip flick of his head when Van was in speaking distance, and a smile appeared within the ragged beard, a tool of truce.

"Can you do me a favor, dude?" the man said. He squeezed awkwardly into one of the swings, his hands clenching the rusted iron chains. "Push me."

"Push you?" Van said.

"Come on, man. I'm not a pervert. Look around. Shoot."

A number of houses backed onto the park and dozens of windows stared down at them, it was true. Still, Van thought, it was an odd way to make the point.

"I'm Sasquatch," the man said, reaching forward to offer his hand. "It's a nickname."

"Hi." Sasquatch's hand was doughy and warm from his pocket.

"Come on, just for a little bit. I forget how to get it going."

"You just kick your legs. How could you forget?"

"Indulge me, man," Sasquatch said. "What's it gonna cost you?"

He smiled. Van walked around behind him. Sasquatch wore a heavy old army coat, and Van placed his hands on the man's shoulder blades. Sasquatch tensed his body to accept the energy just as Van leaned and shoved and had the thought that Sasquatch had done this before. The man was on his way.

Van pushed him perhaps a dozen more times, heaving him forward and backing out of the way to avoid the return swing. Sasquatch was silent in flight, the wind inflating his jacket and parting his beard and hair. The chains of the swing set screeched like birds in pain. When the lunges of the swing brought the chains to parallel with the earth, Sasquatch called, "Enough!" Van stepped back. On the next rush forward, just at the peak of the swing's altitude and acceleration, Sasquatch pushed himself from the seat, continuing up perhaps another four feet in the air, floating there a moment as the swing twisted and jingled and fell away, and then he was sucked back to the earth to splash in the sandbox with a thud Van felt in his feet.

Sasquatch crumbled onto his side, but did not cry out or even grunt. He quickly got up and brushed the sand from his knees.

"Thanks, dude," he said, and walked off.

Van headed home. The house was empty. Brenda was still at work, and Kara was supposed to be at soccer practice but was probably smoking with her friends at the creek. Charlie appeared in the kitchen wagging his stub tail as though expecting Brad; the dog whined at Van and turned away. Van ate an orange, drank milk from the carton, and noticed that one of the refrigerator magnets was missing, another piece of Brad's loot, a small rottweiler's head.

Van wandered out to the garage. The dank two-car was filled with junk, a heaping pile of stuffed boxes and small appliances broken just beyond Brad's knowledge of repair. Van circled the mound.

I am thinking quite well, he thought.

The first piece came from a basketball backboard that Brad had shaped from plywood but never hung over the garage door. The slope of the backboard at its apex matched nicely the curve of a set of imagined shoulders, and Van had only to shear off the edges to give it the rough shape of an armless torso. The old tree saw he used barely managed the knots, and the floor was quickly covered with sawdust. Van sanded the frayed edges of the backboard with his palms, then found a short bit of pipe. He picked through Brad's tackle box of bolts and nuts until he found a match, then screwed the pipe into the board, holding the nut in place with his finger and twisting until he stabbed his own fingerprint. The pipe held. Van had a choice of three Christmas tree stands for a base, and picked the one whose spike fit the pipe best. The torso stood upright at dwarf height, firm and solid, like something built to outlast the generation of its creator.

The next piece was the obvious choice: a Styrofoam wig head. He plucked it from a shelf and the saw tore into it, small bits of Styrofoam flying away like sparks from a difficult weld. The cut was done in seconds, a slit bisecting the base of its neck. Van fastened the head onto the top of the backboard, and the construction came to life now, the head's blank expression fed emotion by the addition of a body at scale.

Van backed away from it just as Kara appeared in the door to the kitchen. She was backlit, hair bound in pigtails that cut her age by a third. She stood on one leg, posing.

"Oh, God," she said. "What are you doing?"

"I don't know," Van said.

She stepped down into the garage. "What is it?"

Van opened his mouth to speak, but then thought that words would ruin whatever it was.

"It's a person," Kara decided. "It's Dad."

She wasn't right, but denying it wouldn't help. "There was a man in the park today," Van offered. "I walked home. There was someone I met."

"No," Kara said. "It's Brad. It's Dad." She was quiet a moment, and passed a toe through the layer of sawdust and Styrofoam bits on the cement floor. "Rice and corn," she said.

They were quiet in miscommunication. The garage filled with the faint sound of the television running in the far-off living room.

"It's a manikin," Brenda said later, when Kara dragged her into the garage after she'd come home from work. "What the hell's it for?"

Van, hands at his sides, shrugged. He liked the word—*manikin*.

"He's going to make it a girl," Kara tried now. "He's going to give it tits."

Brenda reached out to jostle the manikin, test its buoyancy. The figure had two sections of flimsy plastic tubing for arms now, and they wagged in tandem at Brenda's touch. "That true?"

"It's not a woman," Van said.

Brenda's eyes stayed with the manikin a moment. "Whatever," she said, and went inside.

The next day, Kara was already home when Van returned from school. Again he had walked, but today the park was empty. He stood before the shrine of the refrigerator, and

Kara passed behind him carrying a large shovel, her feet trailing dirt from the backyard.

"What are you doing?" he asked.

"A project," she said, headed for her room. "Like your doll."

Silence solved the proclamation. It was Charlie. The dog had not appeared to investigate him. Brad's .22 leaned against the wall next to the sliding glass door that led out to the backyard. Its barrel was warm. Van stared out into the yard, but everything was the same. Back in the family room, Kara splayed herself across the sofa to read biology.

In the garage, Van unwound several coat hangers and threaded them through the manikin's arms to give them a stiff elbowish bend. One he turned slightly in, and the other he brought all the way up to the belly as though the manikin was about to check the time on a pocket watch. He found a brass back scratcher whose business end was a small clawed hand. He snapped it in Brad's vise, then wound it into the manikin's arm until it protruded just right. A kitchen implement became the other hand, some kind of prodder or scooper, and when it was in place it took imagination to see it as a hand even mildly deformed. But it was right.

He was digging in the pile for features for the manikin's face when he heard the phone ring. Brenda's shoes clacked across the kitchen plastic, and Van heard the pitch of her voice but not her words. In a moment, she appeared in the door.

"There's someone on the phone named Derek Finger. Your English teacher, right?"

"Yes," Van said.

"He says he wants to discuss your grade." She looked the
manikin up and down, eyeing its development. Van realized
that he wanted it to please her. "But he's just hitting on
me, right?"

"Probably."

Brenda's face collapsed into consideration, recalling
parent nights at school. "He's the kind of scrawny one, right?
But cute."

"I guess so. Yeah."

She squinted out past the garage. Then she turned
decisively and clacked back into the house.

✚

Buttons pinned to the head for irises, smaller buttons pinned
to them for pupils. A plastic set of Mr. Potato Head lips fixed
to the mouth. A mop, rank and stiff with old scum, for hair.
An old fedora, a pair of sunglasses, belt buckles for epaulets.
A plaid of expired coupons staple-gunned into the plywood
for a shirt. Another shirt on top of that. The manikin was
Van's height now, legs of the same plastic tubing as its arms,
threaded through a pair of blue jeans Brad had used for
working in the yard. Croquet mallets for feet. Slippers slipped
over them. The manikin began to look comfortable.

Mr. Finger was home one day after school. Van had not
said anything to him in class for several days, and Mr. Finger
had avoided calling on him between writing assignments.
Brenda and Mr. Finger were at tea in the kitchen when Van
arrived home.

"He said something about Tulsa," Van heard Brenda say, as he pushed his bag into the clutter of the closet. "We heard from a lawyer and started getting checks, but who really knows?"

Mr. Finger had his hands wrapped around his teacup as though it were a chalice. He pressed his lips wisely. It was as ridiculous to see him away from his classroom, Van thought, as it would have been to see a monkey loping madly down the street.

"Hi, sweetie," Brenda said.

"Hi, Van," Mr. Finger said.

Van nodded.

"Van, show Derek your thing out there," Brenda said, nodding toward the garage. Then, to Mr. Finger, "He's working on the most interesting thing. He's so smart! What is it, anyway, honey?"

"It's a manikin," Van said.

"I'd be happy to take a look," Mr. Finger said. "Maybe we can give you some extra credit there, huh?"

"Give me a minute."

Van went out to the garage. The manikin wasn't done. He had come to realize that he was ashamed that he cared what others thought about it. He had gone to the park every day since that first, but he had not seen Sasquatch again.

Kara entered the garage through the door that led to the side yard. "Oh," she said. She was struck by the sight of the manikin—she hadn't seen it since height had given it power. She stared for a moment and recovered.

"That's your teacher in there, right?" she said.

"Yeah," Van said. He began to sift through the pile for

something to make the manikin perfect before Mr. Finger came through the door.

"I just read in an article today," Kara said, "where women whose husbands take off sometimes get really promiscuous all of a sudden. It has to do with natural selection and spreading the genome."

Van scanned for metaphor in the entrails of a blender. "Did you really kill Charlie?"

Kara smiled. "I took a shot at him. But I missed. He ran away. The little fucker had an escape planned the whole time. I filled in his hole so he can't come back."

Mr. Finger knocked on the door from the kitchen. "Can I come—out?" he called.

Kara rolled her eyes.

"Yeah," Van said.

"It's art," Mr. Finger said, after descending to the floor of the garage and taking a moment to examine the manikin. "We should get you talking to Mr. Reginald."

"I heard Mr. Reginald's a fairy," Kara said.

"That's not nice," Mr. Finger said.

Van did not want to talk to Mr. Reginald and he now regretted showing the manikin to anyone. The next moment was awkward for all of them. Kara left again through the side door without a word.

"Well," Mr. Finger said, "thanks for showing me your piece, Van." He climbed back into the house to where Brenda was waiting.

✚

Van colored the face of the manikin blue with airplane model paint. Then he decided blue was the wrong color. He tried yellow to cover it, but it all started to turn green, and he stopped. He put the manikin's eyes back in, its glasses and lips. He changed the position of its arms so that they were raised in a pose of surrender. It made the manikin look frightened, but there was nothing he could do about it.

He finally saw Sasquatch again at a convenience store. The man behind the counter said "Hey, dude" when Van approached with a soda and a candy bar. Van looked at him closely. The man was clean shaven and his hair was cut, but it could have been Sasquatch cleaned up for the job, and his badge said TRAINEE. Van looked into his eyes as the man counted out the change, but there was only routine in the brief hospitable glance Van was granted before the next customer pushed up behind him. Still, it was enough of a look for Van to know that the manikin was a failure.

Brenda had a date with Mr. Finger that night. Van and Kara watched television as she prepared. Once she came out from the bedroom wearing a slip to ask her daughter's preference between two dresses.

"The black one's sluttier," Kara said.

Brenda wore the black. She touched her hair in the mirror near the front door as the minutes ticked down to Mr. Finger's arrival. "Everything's changed now, guys," she called to them. "I'll be back late."

When the car pulled into the drive, she left before Mr. Finger could come into the house.

"I don't like this," Kara said.

They watched television together for the rest of the night, until its bright signals punctured them and made them weary and became the flickering light of the house. Black settled across the neighborhood, and soon they were as tired and stiff as if they had lived the petty dramas unfolded before them. Kara had made some French fries, and the ravaged plate sat on the coffee table between them. Van had left the last of them for his sister, but she had done the same for him, and now it sat as lonely monument to their new cooperation.

"You're not working on your doll," Kara said, as though the hours of television had not happened at all.

"It's not a doll," Van said. "It's a piece."

"A piece of what?"

"A piece of art. A piece of everything else." Van had the remote and flashed through several channels, flipping past body parts: a flexed thigh, a bare breast, a hand. "Anyway, it's done."

"Really?"

He nodded at the screen, and Kara got up and walked to the garage. She was only gone a minute.

"I don't like it," she said.

Van didn't say anything.

"I'm sorry," she said. "It's almost one o'clock. Mom's not home."

"She said she would be late. It makes sense."

"I guess it does," Kara said. She smiled. "What do you think she's doing *right now*?"

"I don't know."

"I'm going to bed," Kara said.

Van had sat through most of an episode of a generation-old detective drama when he heard the noises in the garage. The tense mood of the television show edging toward its climax climbed out from the box, and the dark world of the house filled with its goofy portent. Sounds like rats, sounds like opossums rooting through refuse. Van tensed, and his mind began to churn pleasantly, and he realized that the flush of quickened thought he had experienced when Brad left had faded, and only returned to him now with the danger.

I am thinking well, he thought again.

He imagined first that it was Charlie returned home, looking for scraps, then, more fantastically, that it was the manikin somehow come to life despite his failure to make it whole. He retrieved the .22 from its spot against the wall, where it had stood since he last touched it. He did not know whether it was loaded, but hefted it in what he hoped was the proper way and walked toward the garage.

It was Brad. The door from the kitchen opened silently, and Van's father was caught near the back of the garage looking through its central heap, just then deciding on an item to set silently into a large canvas bag already half full of pilfered goods. In a moment Brad noticed the light and his son standing above him with a rifle. The manikin stood between them, facing away from Van like a conspirator in the confrontation.

Brad had grown a beard. "You caught me," he said.

Van climbed down the steps to the garage floor, training the rifle generally ahead of him but not exactly pointing it. "Mom's gone."

"I know," Brad said. "I'm glad she's moving on."

"What are you doing?"

Brad looked around the garage as though his chore should be apparent. "I'm cleaning up a bit. What did you think I was doing?" He watched Van's reaction, and gestured at the manikin between them. "You made this, didn't you? A scarecrow. Almost worked. I nearly pissed my pants when I walked in here."

Scarecrow. "Actually, it's art."

"Art? I don't know. As art, I think it needs something."

"Maybe what it needs," Van said, "is in your bag."

Brad looked down at his bag. He looked odd with his new beard, scruffy and younger and dangerous, and somehow it allowed him to remain silent.

"How's Tulsa?"

"Tulsa," Brad said, "is over. I'm headed to Miami."

"Miami," Van said, "is 'I maim' spelled backward."

Brad squinted and walked around the mound. "You better give me that rifle."

Van turned it around like a knife and handed it to him. Brad held the rifle in one hand and his sack in the other like a hunter with a dead turkey. He looked into his son's eyes for a moment with a weird glimmer of transcendence and good-bye. It was important not to look away, and Van held the stare until Brad nodded again at the manikin.

"Take that thing apart," he said. "You're not scaring anyone."

Then he ducked through the side door and out into the world.

CARLSON'S TEAM

In the beginning, television simulated reality. Now it's the other way around. I feel happiest when it seems that I have made it to syndication, when the events in my life that used to occur weekly begin to run every day, early prime.

The Cold Open. I come home from work: rote entrance, enthusiastic applause. I find five packages of men's briefs on the hall table. A simple event unrelated to the plot sets the comedic tension running, and no one gets lost.

"What's this?" I say, believably.

Wendy, my wife, is on the couch, pregnancy comically exaggerated. She watches, in an effect of ironic doubling, a sitcom from the old days: the actors' clothes and hair are twenty years out of style. "It's underwear, stupid," she says. "That's what I did today. Put some on."

She is a mix of the Irritant and the Supportive Parent. She uses a phrase of the day. A predicament—her pregnancy— makes her cranky. Which is funny.

I obey, offstage. The new underwear fits tightly, though it is my size. The elastic cuts, and I feel and look in the mirror as though I am wearing a diaper. I handle the ring of fat, thick as a football, around my waist.

"Shee-oot," I say. Producers smile, censors cringe.

Back downstairs, the set is the same. Familiar locations and limited physical action eliminate the need for elaborate description. Crickets suggest night.

"Where's all my old briefs?" I say.

Wendy does not look away from the television. "They're gone. Don't argue with me. There were stains I don't even want to *discuss*."

Laughter on the television set, laughter in the studio. In the upper dark hide teams of skilled thespians, graduates of seminars on the contagion quotient of giggling.

I join Wendy and the seven-and-a-half-month fetus on the couch. I am the Infant Clown. The premise: average, emotionally undeveloped professional adopts eating and television habits of pregnant wife, and gains weight along with her. Joke sequences follow easily as the story's dramatic tension is organic and rich.

I push a finger into the elastic band of the underwear and create a small tent of relief. "It's like needles," I say, whiny, "all around my waist."

"I empathize," Wendy says.

"Women must not experience things like this." The inconsiderate husband, spittle thick with testosterone.

She grabs my hand and runs it across the huge balloon of her belly, which she leaves uncovered at home. "Believe me, we have it worse."

"But these are cotton, right? They're gonna get smaller, even."

The Triple: setup, setup, punch line. Exploit the literal.

"You're the one who should be getting smaller," Wendy says.

I purse my lips, accept my due humiliation until the purgative psychical energy that results from aggressive humor is fully discharged. We are quiet then, slipping toward the first commercial break. I move behind my wife, splaying my legs around her as though for a bizarre manner of intercourse. In the process of rapid growth, Wendy's navel has completely inverted itself so that now it protrudes like a third nipple, her belly a giant extra breast. I reach around and finger the tender knob.

She ignores me, and clicks the television to a show about World War II bombing raids. Aerial footage of black-and-white explosions flowering over buildings and railroad tracks as a Brit lists statistics of downed Allied flight crews. Sitcoms are not about abortion debates or the Holocaust. Goals and strategies are often silly, and the stakes are usually small. The explosions on the television come with soft, overlaid burping sounds, and after a moment Wendy begins to make a similar noise, reacting to my touch.

"That feels nice," she says. "Go lower."

I obey. Were it only a show, we would fade to a miraculous black. I touch her between her legs as the air war escalates, then recall a dream sequence. My blank eyes searching stage left distorted by the wavy lines of affordable special effects launch a transition to an alternate temporal space: Wendy dies during childbirth. The cartoonish blood from ketchup packets articulates my intense emotion of being ill-equipped to assist the obstetric team working to save her. The surgical gowns are all properly pea-colored, but the instruments are implements from our kitchen. The baby is not in the sequence at all, and the deerlike glaze that coats Wendy's eyes upon death makes me wake crying, tucked ironically into a fetal position, my pillow damp with tears and spit.

Misery serves as half the setup. Sad, universal truths are comic and episode-worthy. If movies are larger than life, then sitcoms are smaller. Which is funny.

$$\oplus$$

A joke may say what it has to say by not saying it: avoid surplus information. Comedy has precision.

I work at the widget factory: there are a dozen departments (legal, accounting, marketing, production, shipping, and so on) whose varying compensation budgets are like a socioeconomic ladder describing the culture. The workforce's blend of individuals with dissimilar social skills, family traditions, educational backgrounds, intelligence levels, and eating habits spawns riotous conflict of misunderstanding.

Act I. I sign up for the company basketball league, the poster for which I find pinned to the coffee room bulletin board. I am thinking of shedding pounds. It's five weeks from Wendy's due date, and I tell myself that if I start now I can lose the equivalent of a baby and a placenta by that same day. The Time Bomb: a character enters a predicament in which he must accomplish an impossible goal by a fast-approaching deadline.

I forget about the league by that afternoon.

Flash to three days later. Wendy and I are again before the television. The evening's string of comic humiliations has played out before us, and we are now rewatching the fetus's six-month sonogram. Five little fingers transparent as yarn, eyes oblong dark slugs. Its legs are crossed with its shy secret.

Brr-ring.

It's Jacobs, a widget vice president, a man whose photo I have seen but whom I have never met. He makes a hasty introduction—visiting characters do not outshine series regulars—and begins the interrogation.

"How tall are you, Carlson?"

"Five-ten," I say.

"Weight?"

"Uh . . . two-fifteen."

Insert Wendy's exaggerated take. Extreme circumstances may call for a double take. I shrug funnily. Jacobs pauses in the split screen to write the information down. He is a balding man, athletic, but no giant himself.

"You play any organized ball? High school? College?"

"No. I'd really just like to lose a little weight."

Another moment of pause, this one absent the heft of far-off scribbling. "First game's Sunday night. Wear a red shirt and put a number on it."

A race to see who hangs up first. I lose. I look back at the television, the shady twitching blur of my progeny.

Wendy's sustained take dissolves to a suspicious smile. "Who was that?"

"Work. I joined a basketball league."

"You don't play basketball, Carlson." How funny that she addresses me by my surname, the running gag intact from our pilot and title. "And you're definitely not two-fifteen."

"Shush."

I eject the sonogram and turn the television to a preseason professional basketball game. It's research. The Fish Out of Water: a character enters a world where he does not belong either to impress someone or to get something he cannot have. I retrieve my basketball from the closet, an old underinflated thing that I once received as part of a supermarket promotion. Wendy and I watch the game, baffled, and play catch.

During halftime, Wendy holds the ball alongside her belly: the spongy bladder and her uterus are roughly the same size. We laugh, and the eventual unveiling of the foreshadowed beat will provide a satisfying reward, or, on the other hand, the unresolved line will add a fresh sense of reality. I motion for the ball, and Wendy tosses it to me. I slip it beneath my shirt and take a few steps around the room, bowlegged. Extra comedy can be extracted through the temporary exchange of character roles, and Wendy's giggles follow the contagion quotient. I plop down next to her, infected myself, and feel the ball as if for a baby's kick, a delicate sounding or divination. Then the real fetus kicks, and Wendy winces. She lifts her gown and we watch the skin move in close-up, the quickened life beneath it already begging attention. I put my hand on the spot, to soothe it.

The Button: a clever line or small dramatic twist at the end of a scene that provides closure before moving on to the next assignment.

✪

I choose for myself the number 25, the date in October on
which the fetus is due. I make the shapes on a thin shirt from
college that was once red but is now a dark pink. Some comic
visuals do not involve physical injury.

The team is already gathered in the gym when I arrive.
They are widget employees, representatives of the various
departments, an economically diverse sampling of ambitious
manhood. There is Phipps from marketing, a lanky older
gent with a propensity for creative puns, Dickinson and
Thomas from production, broad-shouldered men who
whisper racial humor and laugh out loud, Rivers from the
loading dock, our young African American ringer who smiles
constantly, and of course Jacobs, whose office is next to the
president's and who finds nothing even remotely humorous.
Which is funny.

I am from accounting.

We shoot around for ten minutes before the game, falling
eventually into a disorganized layup drill. Two minutes before
game time, Jacobs calls us around the bench and hands out
a playing schedule made up on perforated computer paper.
I see at once how he has figured it. Five players on the floor,
four quarters in a game: twenty player-quarters. There are
six members of our team, so divide twenty by six to arrive
at 3.3 quarters each. Jacobs rounded down and awarded the
extra quarters to himself and Rivers. I am scheduled to play
quarters one, two, and three.

Choose a hip and catchy tune to accompany montage of first game. Add tape of riotous laughter as benign but inept protagonist makes two "turnovers" in the first quarter (Phipps, tapping my stomach: "As in, too many apple turnovers, Champ!") and is penalized for something called "three-seconds" in the second quarter (Dickinson to Thomas, "His wife calls him for the same damn thing!"). My one shining moment is not even mine: I pass the ball to the fluidly darting Rivers, who drives the lane and scores. Follow us up the court, two men with little in common backpedaling in sync. Close slow-motion as Rivers extends his hand for the acknowledgment of a fine pass; the touch is between a shake and a caress, a respect communicated wordlessly so as to conserve precious energy. Fish Out of Water's exhausted expression: exercise and an unlikely intimacy make the moment and the game vastly rewarding.

Eventually, my man—the man I guard—becomes a camera-trick flash. I pull myself in favor of Phipps halfway through the third quarter and watch the remainder from the bench, confused but fascinated. The buzzer at the end of the game frightens me, and I do a slapstick tumble. I recover as my team returns to the bench downtrodden, some of them limping, towels draped over their bodies like shawls. Close on the protagonist as he glances at the scoreboard and realizes that his team has lost by thirty points.

My disappointment is short-lived. I drive home excited. My muscles are taut and ready for more action, and the cool, raspy sting of my jersey on the car seat is enjoyable and even arousing. At home, I kiss the wife and head for the bathroom.

I urinate and step on the scale: three pounds gone as though from miscarriage.

✛

Act II. A week before the next game. The droll roll of suburban time is conveniently expressed by the temporal compression practiced in basic situation comedy construction.

I go to the library, where a book explains the rules of basketball, including the "three-seconds" violation that got such a laugh in Act I. The book has a good deal to remember, but protagonist is a Clown, not an idiot: I fit it all into a neat mnemonic, a trick learned from working with numbers. Next, I buy a pump, inflate my ball, and perform dribbling drills on the back porch, dribbling with one hand without looking, dribbling with my bad hand without looking, feeling a surge of panic whenever the ball, which wasn't ever round, takes a bounce that isn't true and shoots away into the grass. Finally, for three afternoons straight, I drive to the high school, to the metal-backboard courts behind the swimming pool, and I work on my shot, concentrating, as the book has instructed, on form. The ball makes a heavy satisfying chunk when it splashes through the chain net, and I begin to make as many as I miss. Sometimes, the ball catches a spin on the net that steers it right back to me. These are the best—when the arc of the shot and the bounce of the return complete a circle, a simplistic resolution. On each afternoon, I stay at the courts until sunset, taking shots off the backboard, taking free throws in case I am ever fouled, and occasionally tossing up an offering from behind the three-point line, shots that of course miss the rim, but that sometimes, in the late dim light, look to have been perfect, to have passed through net and rim both without touching them at all.

Our next opponent is a group of five Asian men from the lab, all of whom wear black. Where my team sports numbers like 23, 33, and 32—the numbers of famous professional players, I have come to realize—the black team's numbers are simply 1, 2, 3, 4, and 5. I arrive half an hour early for the warm-up and note the feel of the wooden gymnasium floor, so different from the playground asphalt. When Jacobs arrives, I discover that my playing time has been honed down to fifteen minutes—the last nine of the second quarter, and the first six of the third quarter.

Close on my take. Focus on my dreams, flaws, weaknesses. A character should face the same problems the audience faces, and he should be anything but perfect. Fifteen minutes, I tell myself, is more than enough time to prove my new, practiced worth.

When I enter the game, the first thing I do is dribble the ball off my foot and watch it trickle slowly out of bounds. The black team sees that I am weak and lays off me to double-team Rivers. At halftime, it is still close, the black team ahead by only three points thanks to two dramatic bombs from Jacobs in the final minute.

During intermission, the players line up at the drinking fountain. Jacobs pulls me aside after I wet my lips. He is the Adversarial Mentor, and the tension of our relationship adds a synergistic potency that is subtle, but significant.

"Listen, when you're holding the ball just use your fingertips," Jacobs says, miming the motion with his hands. "That way they can't slap it away with a jackhammer."

He smiles, nudges my arm gently, and walks back to the bench.

I make no important plays during my six minutes in the third quarter. But I do not lose the ball, either. Nor, on the defensive end, does my man score a bucket. I come out of the game breathing hard, and the wooden bench is a haven for my beat legs and knees. Despite twenty-three points from Rivers—sixteen in the second half—the black team wins the game with a fourth-quarter surge. My teammates, dejected by the loss, disperse quietly to the parking lot and their separate cars.

Back to the studio and live audience. Wendy is in bed, thumbing the October *Baby*, sheets veiled over her massive gut. On the television is the premiere of a new series, the adventures of a classic anti-family whose arguments, backbiting, and betrayals generate riotous premise-driven comedy. I strip and shower, and climb beneath the sheets into a womblike space with the fetus. There is a fine yellow glow there that pulses as the characters move on the television screen, like clouds passing before the sun. I place my hand on Wendy's dislocated hip. We quit intercourse a month ago, when it became painful for her. I didn't like the image of it anyway: pressing the fetus, prodding it.

Wendy peels across a slick magazine page. "How was the game?" she says, as four feet away hate makes for laughs.

"We lost. By twelve, I think."

"Did you score any points?"

"No."

I grow restless in utero. I worm my way up Wendy's side until I can put my lips between her shoulder blades, a portion of her recognizable despite the metamorphosis. After the birth she will be forever changed, I think, but even if I lose my fat I will be only the same as before. What had once seemed similar is now revealed as incongruous, a compounding of predicaments.

"I don't think they like me," I say.

"Who?"

"My team. No one really talks to anyone. Or to me, anyway. It's all just about the game."

"Do *I* have to explain men to *you*?" Wendy says, but the joke's flaw is the lack of contrast in its straight line. "I thought you liked it. Anyway, you just wanted to lose weight."

"And I have," I say. "I'd just like to know someone's first name."

The running gag appears again, retooled.

Wendy rolls over, an inefficient maneuver like a seal moving on dry land. She tucks my hair behind my ears. "Masturbate," she says. "You'll feel better."

I am emerged from the womb now, born. I let my head fall back against the pillow. "They cut my playing time."

Wendy makes a sour face and leans in to kiss my chest, once at the base of my throat, once down some. "Poor baby," she says.

"I know I'm not very good. But they could have asked me."

She begins a shift toward the bottom of the bed, pausing to lick my stomach just above the line of fat. Her swollen breasts press against my thighs, and for a moment I have that hackneyed feeling that I am in bed with a stranger. My eyes find the television, where domestic dysfunction and casual violence shape an inadvertent bit of rhetoric: is the show mirror or crystal ball? Prediction, reflection, fate? Wendy finds my waist, taking a majority of the sheets with her, and though I have already responded to her touch and intention, my mind and eyes are focused on the screen, the comic roller-coaster of spite, anger, and happy endings.

"I guess they've got to do what's best for the team," Wendy whispers, and then goes quiet in the conduct of her sloppy chore.

✚

The factory hits high gear the following week. There's a run on widgets, it's widget season, the country is plagued by a shortage of widgets. Higher widget sales means more money, bigger numbers. I have always thought of numbers in terms of literal length, from left to right. The numbers coming in now are both long and abstractly big, which presents a kind of double challenge. The stakes go up, jeopardy mounts, and tension increases geometrically.

Little time for thoughts of either basketball or the approaching fetus. Both go on fine without me. Jacobs gathers the team for a Wednesday-night practice I am forced to skip, and Wendy expects to turn any day. On Saturday night, I am visited by another dream sequence: Wendy again, in a sports shirt made red by the matter of her womb, spread wide on the birthing chair. She cheers emphatically through the ordeal, and when the child comes its face has no features but is marked with rubber seams.

Act III. I go to the third game grudgingly, not yet rested from the trial of the previous week. I step into the gym four minutes before tip-off, just as my team begins a complicated pregame passing drill. Their movements are sped up in the camera, or so it seems, their skills so far beyond me now that even the physics appears warped. I try to follow but become dizzy. Which is funny. As well, my team has acquired new uniforms without me—baggy jerseys with white fabric numbers steampressed into the cotton. On the bench is a stack of playing schedules. Jacobs has done it on a laser printer this time, complete with colored pie charts and bar graphs, various offensive and defensive schedules predicted with a math beyond my training. My name appears only once on the page:

(A) Carlson

Jacobs appears at my shoulder, slowed to normal time, as I examine the sheet. He has on new shoes: the white leather is wrapped around itself like an exposed musculature and there is a hard pocket of air caught in the sole for added bounce.

"We got you a shirt," he says. "Extra-large. 25. I left it at home, though."

"What does 'A' mean?"

"Alternate."

"So when do I come in?"

"You don't necessarily. If someone gets hurt or sick, then you play."

"And if everything goes well?"

"Then you stay here."

Jacobs relaces one of his high-tech shoes, wrapping the cords once around his ankle, and heads back onto the floor. I sit numbly on the bench until my team and our opponents, dressed in blue, shake hands and begin.

The royal "we" build toward the key dramatic moment that is located, 90 percent of the time, in the block comedy scene. My team is better without me is the realization. There is among them now a sense of cohesion and singularity, a confidence and pride that comes from a unity of purpose. The ball moves between them along wires, and the hissing sound effect of its speed may only be my imagination. Instead of improving my skills, I realize, my attempts to master the game have resulted in only a more complete appreciation of just how poor I am it. The game stays close. The blue team, similarly engaged with one another, keeps three men on the bench who shout phrases of support as I sit silently. They are my further failure, as the injection of fresh legs into the game will take its toll on my team: our loss will be my fault even if I never play.

Second-level predicaments happen in real time: seven minutes into the second quarter, Phipps shoots up near the rim for a rebound and comes down on someone's foot. He collapses to the floor with a scream that lasts long enough to melt into the gymnasium's echo. Phipps comes to the bench on the shoulders of Jacobs and Thomas. I do not need to be told that I will enter the game, and none of my teammates look at me as we walk out onto the floor.

The man I cover—a trucker from shipping—is barely human: six-five, thin like stretched taffy, fingers wrapped around the ball with an apparent extra joint. I once nick his pass, wholly by accident, so that it goes out of bounds. On the offensive end, I hustle through the key, careful to avoid three seconds inside it. The shrill whistles of the referees and the bird shrieks of the shoes on the wood prove disorienting, and before long I lose track of which basket is ours and which is not. On one trip down the court, I notice my skinny shadow— my man—following me, and see that Jacobs has the ball, dribbling above the foul line. For a moment, it looks as though he is going to pass it to me, and I put my hands out as though it were a thrown child, a life-or-death bundle. But when the ball leaves his hands it takes a different trek, disappearing as if in a magic trick. I swish pan around, but it is gone, lost in an unfocused blue and red wash of players bounding and blocking out, and so I look up, as the one thing I have learned is that when the orange flash is missing it is usually in the air. And as though to bring to completion the trick that made it vanish, it reappears, falling into my hands like a surprised pigeon or a bouquet of flowers, so fast and unexpected that I forget the hours spent practicing form and concentration, and I shove the ball off with both hands, pushing more than shooting, toward the hoop. Tight and silent on the basket as the ball appears and clatters through the rim.

The blue team leads by six at halftime. With the help of a stiff ankle brace and a thousand milligrams of ibuprofen, Phipps squeezes his swollen foot back into his shoe, ties it airtight, and plays the second half. My two points do not console me. I have failed to even break a sweat, and I sit on the bench for the remainder of the game, waiting for something more to go awry. My team finds its unity again despite Phipps's immobility, and we win the game on Rivers's shake-and-bake buzzer-beater from the top of the key.

The blue team appears to congratulate us. I shake the hands that appear in front of me. Jacobs gives a short speech, the gist of which is that for the next game we will use the same plan. I put my arms in my jacket and make my way to the parking lot, alone.

Jacobs catches up behind me under a streetlight, a fluorescent tube casting down a cone of hazy orange. He wears no coat, and small wisps of steam rise from his shoulders into the night's chill.

"You filled your role perfectly tonight," my superior says.

I breathe. The Beat: a moment, discovery, or incident that alters the character's goals and cranks up the tension. Action forces reaction.

"It's like you don't want me to play," I say.

Jacobs tosses his head, taken aback. "Well, that's not the case at all. But if you want, I'm sure we can get your league money refunded."

"I didn't say I wanted to quit."

"I didn't say you did. But you should know that without you we are still a fully-complemented basketball team."

"A better team."

"Well, different. Without you, we would have forfeited tonight."

"I feel like you're selling me a car."

As though on cue, a black minivan glides up beside us, Jacobs's ride. The windows are tinted, but I see Phipps at the wheel and sense the rest of my team inside.

"That makes sense only in that we're talking business. This is business," Jacobs says. He climbs in the passenger door, and nods. "See you Sunday." Which is funny.

○

The front yard: black light, the faux crickets, the distant recorded dog. I turn on a garden hose and run a few handfuls of hard water through my hair so it will appear that I have exerted myself.

The Tag: a very quick final scene tossed in just for laughs, as the story line has been resolved at the end of the last act. Inside, Wendy is awake yet, reclined on the sofa and naked from the waist up. She is rubbing one of her breasts with a coarse scouring pad. The television runs another new series: the action-packed lives of a gang of diverse and privileged high schoolers. I pause at the mouth of the room to survey my scant realm: Wendy, bare before me, hair falling around her shoulders, shiny in the television light.

"I need you for something," she says.

I move toward her, staring at the scouring pad. "What are you doing?"

"I'm toughening my nipples so I can nurse. Otherwise, they'll crack and bleed."

"You could use a breast pump and bottle-feed."

"Yeah, right. Like I need *those* consequences."

"No-tit is worse than hind-tit?"

"You got it. Come over here. You're not smelly, are you?"

I approach the couch, wishing I were smellier. "What do you want me to do?"

She pushes her chest forward. "What do you think?"

"Won't milk come out?"

She looks off to mentally consult the relevant text. "Breasts don't produce anything until birth. A yellowish, mucuslike liquid called colostrum comes first, and lasts several days. Then you get lactation."

I shrug, and slide onto the couch. Wendy is freakish now, as though in a daredevil feat she's managed to swallow a bowling ball dropped from a great height—perhaps it was this thought that inspired the appropriate prop. I put my hands on my wife's breasts. There are mats of wiry red marks from the scouring pad. The hormones have made her sensitive, and her nipples go hard just from the touch.

"Couldn't I just manipulate them?" I say. "Give them a couple good pinches?"

"No. Take your medicine. And don't pull any punches. Babies have no mercy."

Which is funny. I take to the business. After a minute, I kick off my shoes and begin to enjoy the soothing, sexless affection of it. The voices of the television—the horrific teenybopper dates, the jocks who pester nerds without the dire consequences—fade into a jumble of useless language, but set the mood for my own humbling life. Everywhere my body touches Wendy's is seared with warmth, and I register a flicker coming from her, a passionate quiver that I recognize

soon enough as the sputter of a double heartbeat. It brings
the cliché thought that I will be a father soon, and that, like
basketball, I will be good at it only sporadically, and with luck.

"Am I doing this right?"

"Suck harder," Wendy says. "Pretend you're hungry. You
haven't said anything about the game."

"We won."

"Did you score?"

"I'm scoring now."

"Ha."

"I scored one basket," I say. "That's two points."

I keep my tongue and teeth working. Close on Wendy's
take as she writhes beneath me. I pass my hand over the
bowling ball, impossibly warm, and feel it struggle beneath
my fingers: the fetus is anxious to emerge, and, as with
laughter, nervous excitation tends to beget muscular motion.
I speak with my mouth full.

"What if I'm no good at it?"

"Men always think they're no good," Wendy says. "It's just
a game."

But it's miscommunication, and the gag falls flat. I switch
breasts, and run my hand to Wendy's pelvic bone, across the
heat of her bloated frame.

DALRYMPLE

We gave ourselves a warning sign about Dalrymple—we
refused to call him doctor—but we didn't heed it, so it's fair
to say we brought this on ourselves. He wasn't the kind of
guy that put you on the lookout for red flags. Beederman
remembers—or says he remembers—Dalrymple's mobile
laboratory pulling into town that first day, a converted ice
cream truck with the speaker still on the roof, the whole
thing painted lab coat white, the sides festooned with letters:

Dr. Darymple's Amazing "Sleep" Machine

Thing was, Dalrymple didn't strike anyone as the
authoritative type, let alone a medical doctor. He was a
messy-haired guy with a mustache to hold back an ocean
with and a sweat gland problem. A momma's boy type. Sort
of guy you'd offer loose change if he'd looked just a bit more
down on his luck.

He set up shop at the mall. Scenic had just the one, a
great big structure, 467 stores, though most of them are
empty now. Dalrymple found space in one of the piazzas—
level two, near the playground—and he brought in, all by
himself, a pair of the compartments, as he called them,

big space age-looking things, crossed between a diving bell and an astronaut suit. Later, we would see more advanced versions of the compartments, but that first pair were like patched-together prototypes, his and hers whatevers, and Tiptoft wonders why no one ever asked to see a permit for the things, which, even as they looked as though Dalrymple had put them together in the back of his ice cream truck, did look like a complicated bit of machinery. Others say Dalrymple's goofball manner prevented questions. He just didn't look like a guy who knew the answers.

We ignored him at first; we ignored him for a long time. The children, not surprisingly, were the first to pay him mind, raising stubby fingers to Dalrymple's freestanding sandwich board and demanding a translation.

1/2 HOUR—$10

2 HOURS—$25

1 DAY—$200

???—PLEASE INQUIRE

Which of course their parents could not provide, except to say that it seemed some kind of service was being exchanged for money. Dalrymple didn't exactly come on with a hard sell. He sat there reading our local newspaper—the *Scenic Whig-Herald*, owned and operated by the Lions Club—ignoring those who stopped to puzzle over the sign. He came and went every day, loading and unloading the compartments, driving the ice cream truck to and from who knows where. Dalrymple appeared to have nowhere else to go and an unflappable patience. The patience, Hasselbeck now says, of a hungry fisherman.

Which eventually paid off. The first to bite was Pitzl-Waters, who later admitted that the idea to give Dalrymple a try came after he and a few friends finished watching a football game. They were liquored up, their team had won, the night was young, and Scenic was not exactly brimming with resources for celebration. Pitzl-Waters himself suggested Dalrymple, who by that time was a town fixture. Dalrymple, Pitzl-Waters said, was the only adventure they had, and the mall was still open.

Dalrymple met the four men not like a vendor greeting his first customers in months, but with the annoyance of a shopkeeper staying open five minutes extra after a long day. Pitzl-Waters didn't care. He giggled the whole time Dalrymple fixed him up with sensor pads. Pitzl-Waters opted for just the half-hour plan, so his pals were still drunk when Dalrymple cracked open the compartment again on that first occasion. There was no hiss, no escape of pressurized gas to hint at how the machine worked, just a lifting of the lid and a peculiar smell—wet cardboard—that we never have been able to figure out.

Pitzl-Waters had sobered on the inside. Which is not to say that he came out refreshed—it's not like that—but certainly he'd gone through some kind of shift. It wasn't like time passing, he told his pals, but it wasn't like no time had passed, either. Rather, it was as though he'd stepped from one era directly into another—another, he said, he was surprisingly ready for.

Now Pitzl-Waters was not a man to come out lightly with a word like *era*. Neither age nor epoch were regular tenants in the storehouse of his vocabulary. Like most of us, he thought about last week and next week, and that was already a lot to handle, and so the others were taken aback by Pitzl-Waters's talk of an era-making machine. Yes, they said, but what was it like? Should they try it themselves? Was it dangerous? How many brain cells had he lost?

"It was like," Pitzl-Waters said, "being off."

"Off?"

"Turned off. Like a light."

"Did you dream? Were you just asleep?"

Pitzl-Waters was certain about this. "No."

Most of those who came immediately after Pitzl-Waters chose the one-hour plan. The results were predictable: Pitzl-Waters's experience was heightened, though no one, not even Pitzl-Waters, who went back for a second dose, was willing to characterize the hour sleep as twice as good as the half-hour sleep. "Good" didn't quite describe it, and others disagreed with Pitzl-Waters's time talk. The compartments weren't relaxing, particularly. It wasn't like taking a sauna. (The best description would come from Ullyat, who some time later stood up during the public comment portion of a special meeting of city council. "It's like the same thing you're inside of is inside of you," Ullyat said.)

Regardless, Dalrymple began doing a tidy business. He upgraded to the more modern-looking compartments—opaque face plates, flush bolts—added six units, and moved into the alcove of the mall's first failed business, a cookie bakery. People started taking doses on lunch hours, or cut out of work early and hit the mall before dinner. There was generally a line. Dalrymple arranged to stay open as long as the multiplex. A few people tried the daylong plan to get through weekends or lonely holidays—they came out neither hungry nor rested. Dalrymple started taking reservations and gift cards. He moved into a second failed shop, a shoe store. He couldn't keep up with demand, but at least he didn't have to lug the compartments in and out of the mall anymore. The ice cream truck disappeared.

Edna Skym was the first to inquire about the final stage of Dalrymple's treatment sequence—mentioned on his old sandwich board. We all knew about Edna's difficulties—with Fred, her husband, and their neighbor, Devon Sheach—and Obrissel, who worked as a mall guard, claims that he saw Edna sit down with Dalrymple in the back of the shoe store one day with a stack of papers. She looked a little shaggy, slumped, and resigned. They were still there when Obrissel returned for his second round two hours later. Obrissel didn't see her sign anything, but it was the last any of us saw of her. Sort of.

The next morning Dalrymple had opened another new store, a gutted lingerie outlet up on level four. There was just one compartment in it—Edna Skym's. She was locked inside, or so Dalrymple said, and there was no indication of when she was coming out. Now Sheriff Kjar got interested. He gathered together a couple deputies and lawyers, and wandered over. Dalrymple greeted them warmly, opened his books. Sheriff Kjar pulled him aside while the lawyers sifted through Edna's contract.

"No bullshit—how long's she in there for?" Kjar said.

"She's got a permanent deal, sheriff."

"How much that go for?"

"You'll need a court order for that."

Kjar nodded his frustration—the level-headedness that got him elected. He nodded again when the lawyers admitted that all the paperwork seemed to be in order. They took their leave. The next day two more compartments appeared in the lingerie store—Fred Skym and Devon Sheach, of course. People were uneasy about that, at first. It felt like a murder-suicide, except we never knew who'd been murdered, and who was the suicide.

Dalrymple took on his first employee—Sarah Hornback, nice girl, still with us, out of a job because Fred Skym had owned the cutlery kiosk on level one where she worked. Dalrymple trained her for two days. Basically, she kept records on the gauges that looked out from the compartments' rear ends, so to speak. She was supposed to report to Dalrymple if any of the needles showed anything out of the ordinary, which they never did.

For a while, businesses up around the ex-lingerie outlet saw an increase in incidental traffic because people went out of their way to peek in at the three compartments lined up against the back wall—not that you could see anything. Dalrymple's regular business took a bit of a hit. Then the floodgates shuddered. Professor Vandersteen, who taught English at SCC, published "My Last Class" on the opinion page of the *Whig-Herald*. In it, he ranted. Our offspring were "uncurious," he wrote. As a "culture," we had "written reams

on materialism," but were "illiterate in spirit." The only real
view in Scenic, he complained, was of the artificial lake. Near
the end it became clear that this was more than just a lecture:

```
What we have learned, my friends, is that the
evil queen was not evil, she was pragmatic; the
poison apple was not poisoned, it was medicinal;
and the prince's kiss was not affection, it
was rape and a rude awakening indeed.
```

Professor Vandersteen was secure in the lingerie outlet
before his words hit our driveways. An op-ed alone—even
a moving one—wasn't going to trigger an avalanche, but it
was the shout that cracked the snowcap. Pettygrove recalls
Sheriff Kjar talking up the Vandersteen piece at Piskhaver's
barbershop.

"In ancient times," Kjar quoted by heart, "the only exodus
to a better life was the migration of the dead to the paradise
of a suburban cemetery."

The professor was quoting too, but the sheriff didn't seem
to know it or at least he didn't let on that he knew it. Kjar
signed his own permanent sleep contract that night.

The next morning there was a line outside the mall, people
in tents pitched on the asphalt. Dalrymple couldn't keep
up. For a while he tried alternating between installations
and closings, but within a week he was forced to take on
managers to handle contracts, oversee maintenance and
security, and so on. He rented new spaces, and there were
plenty: the arcade, three gift shops, the theme park gift store,

the eyeglass hut. Shipments of compartments came in at night, men in gray overalls dollying them in through the cargo bays.

The financial services industry spiked as people liquidated assets and bought in. Church attendance skyrocketed, then crashed, and before long you could get a Scenic home for a song. Dalrymple hired more staff, and eventually he was spotted only at brief training sessions for upper-tier execs.

The frenzy lasted a month, and didn't stall so much as run out of feed. The mall management was sleeping by then, and those of us who were left—Dalrymple's army—had to figure out the various systems, heating for now, but we're thinking ahead. No one quite remembers the last time we saw Dalrymple. We've gone on without him. A few more were able to fall asleep—we drew straws—when we figured out the minimum workforce necessary to keep everything monitored. Video surveillance has proved invaluable in this regard. Those of us who remain take turns with shorter rests. Sometimes, we go out for a drive, head up to Scenic Overlook, where our kids used to park and make out. We know now that the city of the dead is foretold by easily diagnosed symptoms. When the signs appear, Necropolis is near. There's regret, surely. Each of us could have wound up on the inside. It leaves a hollow feeling. But, nothing ventured, nothing gained, as they say—and we were not the adventurous types.

SAVAGES

Chuck had been out of high school for nearly a year when Mrs. McDermott fired up a chain saw and cut out a small dark cave in the broad line of acacias that separated her backyard from Chuck's parents'. Chuck watched from the alcove of the upstairs guest room as acacia branches near the ground squirted backward into the thick hedgelike row of trees. Several days later, Chuck spotted Mrs. McDermott again from the alcove, inhabiting the green shadows of her new cave. Kneeled back on her haunches, she cupped one hand by her mouth as if to say something she didn't want to have overheard. Off to one side in the yard, bare-chested, Chuck's father was using a long metal-headed rake to punch air holes in the lawn. He pounded the grass a few times and stopped suddenly. His head made several jerking movements as if to locate an alien sound. He found the hole in the acacia trees and Mrs. McDermott beckoned him toward her with milky hands that stretched into the afternoon light. Chuck's father approached slightly crouched, as if creeping up on an animal he thought could be dangerous, and he peered into the opening, his jaw sliding from side to side. Just as he shaded his eyes to see better, Mrs. McDermott lunged and grabbed the back of his neck. Chuck's father dropped the rake, letting it tip slowly to the ground, and Mrs. McDermott dragged him into the cave, palms wide on his bare back.

Chuck kneeled upright and leaned toward the window. "Holy cow," he said, his breath steaming the glass. He stared at the motionless acacias. After a second, he turned his head and called, "Hey, Mom, come up here for a second."

Chuck's mother yelled back indiscernibly and a moment later the pipes from the kitchen trickled off in the walls. His mother's footsteps climbed the stairs. Chuck heard her enter his room, down the hall. "I'm in here," he said, still looking down at the hole where his father had disappeared.

His mother appeared in the doorway. "What are you doing in here?" she said.

Chuck motioned to the window. "Come and take a look at this."

The guest room contained only a sheetless blue box spring and mattress on a wheeled bed frame and a badly scuffed dresser with a mirror. Chuck's mother walked across the bare room to the alcove. "Down there," Chuck said. He pointed to where the rake lay on the grass.

"What?" his mother said. She wiped her hands on the front of her jeans to dry them and moved to look down the line of his finger. "I don't see anything."

"That hole. See that hole? Dad just went in there. Mrs. McDermott just dragged him in there."

Chuck's mother leaned across the padded seat and set her hand against the set of tall French windows that looked over the backyard. Across the top of the acacias, they could view the upper story of the McDermotts' house. As she stretched across the seat, Chuck saw tiny tendons like nylon twine bulging in his mother's neck.

"He was doing something to the yard," Chuck said. "I watched him walk over. Then she jumped out and nabbed him."

His mother didn't say anything. She looked past him down at the hole and they watched it together until the shadows of the acacia trees, thrown by the sun sinking over the McDermotts' house, made visible progress on the lawn. The acacias were unkempt, as they would be in the wild, the thick branches intertwined like an impossible system of wires and cables; they stood eight feet high, half again as deep, and ran across the entire back border of the property. They had been planted there by the people who lived in the McDermotts' house before the McDermotts.

"Jesus Christ," Chuck said. "What do you think they could be doing down there for so long?"

His mother was silent, concentrating. She opened her mouth, but paused before saying anything. "I don't know," she said. Then she said it again, "I don't know," spacing the words out this time so that Chuck knew she had a better idea than he did.

After several more minutes the bushes rattled and Chuck's father crawled out of the hole on his hands and knees. His face was red and he exhaled as he stood, puffing his cheeks out. He brushed acacia leaves off his bare chest and shoulders and stooped to pick up the rake. He checked his fly, hiked his pants, and continued where he'd left off, punching air holes in the lawn. He did it the way a gorilla would swing a tree branch, starting far in back of him, bringing the rake in a high wild arc over his head. When it hit the ground, grass and dirt flew, and Chuck and his mother could hear it even from behind the glass.

Chuck's father made excuses to be in the backyard in the afternoons for several days after that. Vastly overgrown, the backyard had been neglected since Chuck graduated; the bushes tangled together like the balls of lights they unraveled at Christmas, and the lawn was as deep and shaggy as a lion's mane. Chuck's father set about its repair. One day, he rented a fertilizer spreader and spent an afternoon mowing and fertilizing the grass; another, he weeded, trimmed, and watered the Peter Pan and orange trees on the sides of the yard; on another, he clipped the ice plant invading through a neighbor's fence and cleaned up the acacias a bit; and once, as though to reward himself for his labors, he dug out of the garage his dusty clarinet case and took the instrument onto the lawn to play some of the sexier jazz licks he remembered from college.

As soon as he went out the sliding glass door, Chuck and his mother scurried up to the guest room and hid behind the alcove seat. Chuck's father pulled weeds or fiddled on his clarinet, waiting for Mrs. McDermott to call to him. When she did, he hunched down and duck-walked into the hole, and Chuck and his mother climbed up onto the padded seat to

survey the dark green line of acacias. After two days, Chuck's
mother dug a pair of plastic binoculars from an old box and
sat cross-legged, staring through them. Chuck sat next to
her, his arms wrapped around his knees, watching the acacia
branches near the cave entrance move erratically, slightly
faster than the wind-propelled branches nearby. Occasionally
he looked at his mother, expecting to see some sort of
emotion, but she only adjusted the focus of the binoculars
with the tip of her fingernail and squinted harder into the
small lenses.

She was on the downhill side of beauty, Chuck thought.
She had spindly legs, and small deep lines on her lips. She
had a long nose, but the end of it had curved down and
flattened like a beak. Her arms had tight wrinkles like the
skin of an old plum. Once, in the alcove with him, she took
her eyes away from the binoculars and said, "Savages."

"What?"

"Do they think this is the Stone Age?"

"I don't know," Chuck said, imitating her tone from before.

"They're Pygmies or something? Cavemen?"

They watched until Chuck's father came back out, rolling
his head on his shoulders. He went back to whatever he'd
been doing, the manual lawn mower standing by itself
halfway down a row of uncut grass, the lawn chair and
paperback he'd been reading. By the time he came back in
the house, just as it was getting dark, Chuck and his mother
had returned to their old positions: she smoking and reading
newspapers through bifocals, and Chuck watching reruns of
M*A*S*H, laughing at jokes he knew by heart.

✛

After five days of it, Chuck called up his ex-girlfriend Sharon to tell her the story. "Hi, Sharon," he said when she picked up. "How are you doing? How's Steve?"

"Hi, Chuck," Sharon said. "Hey, I thought I told you not to call here anymore. I thought we had an agreement."

Sharon and Chuck had broken up the summer after he graduated, and now Sharon was dating an ex-classmate of Chuck's who had a three-eight in school and was widely known for his tenaciousness in water polo and lacrosse. Sharon was a year behind Chuck and had a deep, fluid, feline voice. Listening to it when they were dating had made Chuck think she was right about everything and now he thought she might be able to advise him on how to react to this development in his parents' relationship.

"Yeah, I know," Chuck said. "I know. But there's something I've got to tell you about."

He listened to the silence that followed and pictured Sharon with the phone pressed to her ear. He saw her toss her long soft brown hair to one side with her free hand. Or maybe, he thought, she was pausing to swallow a chunk of banana—she ate a lot of fruit. Sometimes, when they'd been dating, Chuck had told Sharon she was herbivorous.

"Okay," Sharon said at last. "What? What is it?"

"It's my dad. You won't believe it. He's messing around with Mrs. McDermott, the lady who lives behind us."

"Wait," Sharon said. "What do you mean exactly by 'messing around'?"

"I mean they do things."

"Things like sex?"

"Yes," Chuck said.

"So they're having an affair."

"I don't know if you'd call it that. They just sort of go in the acacias behind our house."

"I know the ones," Sharon said. Then she said, "Have you seen them? Are you sure they're having sex? Because people jump to conclusions about these things. It gets ugly really fast."

"You're right," Chuck said. "I haven't seen them. But what else could they be doing?"

"I don't know," Sharon said. They paused for a few seconds. Chuck sat at the kitchen counter, looking at the door of the microwave. He heard his father pass by outside with the fertilizer spreader.

"I have to go, Chuck," Sharon said. "Steve's here."

"No, he's not," Chuck said. "He has practice today."

"It got canceled."

"Don't lie to me. Why would it be canceled?"

"I'm not lying," Sharon said. "Here, I'll put him on."

Chuck listened to the phone leave her ear. A male voice came on. "Is this Chuck?" the voice said. At first, Chuck thought it was Sharon doing an impersonation, but then he wasn't sure. After a moment he hung up.

He sat there for a while with his elbows on the counter. The only sound was the high hum of the fluorescent lights in the kitchen. Chuck listened until it was disturbed by a soft chirping noise. He leaned across the counter expecting to find a panicked mouse or maybe even a rat running around on the plastic floor of the kitchen. When he didn't see anything he realized the sound was not a soft one nearby, but a loud one far away.

He climbed off his stool and followed it to the staircase. He tried to go up the stairs deftly and silently, avoiding the steps he knew creaked and spreading his weight evenly on his feet. When he got to the top he realized the sound was his mother crying. Chuck had rarely heard his mother cry. It sounded strange, instinctively terrified, like a peaceful animal fighting off a grim predator.

He walked to the doorway of the guest room and looked in. His mother sat on the alcove seat, facing the window. Her shoulders, slouched and pulled in, jumped with the rhythm of her crying. Her hands covered her eyes and the binoculars sat on the seat next to her. Up close, the crying was loud and high-pitched, sudden bits of a tone of voice she used when angry. It ricocheted off the empty walls.

"Hey," Chuck said.

Her body jumped and she turned around. She put her hand on her chest. "Jesus, you scared me," she said. "I didn't hear you."

Chuck walked the rest of the way to the alcove. He set his hand against the wall and his thumb ran across an empty nail hole. "Are you okay? What's wrong?"

His mother gestured behind her with her elbow and sniffled. "Oh, your father's just doing it with his neighbor's wife again," she said. She tried to smile but her eyes dropped and her head wagged back and forth.

Chuck looked down at the trees. The hole in the acacias was dark. The fertilizer spreader was parked diagonally on the lawn. He touched his mother's shoulder and then crossed his arms on his chest. "What's with the crying? That's new."

"I know," his mother said. "I guess all this just hit me, sort of. I didn't want to believe it, you know? I was trying to be strong." She looked up and Chuck watched tears well in her eyes the way blood comes from the eyes of a horned toad. "I guess I'm going to have to divorce him, huh? I mean, that's what you're supposed to do, right?"

She sucked in air to keep from crying again.

Chuck picked up the binoculars. Out the corner of his eye he saw his mother watching as he looked down at the acacias through the lenses. He moved the binoculars around until he found Mrs. McDermott's cave and then focused until he could see veins on the nearest leaves and small round flower buds. He could see movement, but couldn't make out anything specific. It was like looking through a kaleidoscope—he saw shadowed green leaves that shuffled back and forth revealing bits of tan colors, which he took to be flesh.

"Divorce," he said. He paused and watched the leaves a while longer. "This is uncivilized."

He shifted his gaze up and focused on the top story of the McDermotts' house. The outside of it was white stucco that had rusted orange in thin bands around the windows. He looked into a room through thin yellow curtains. There was a dark wood dresser, a small white-painted vanity, and half an unmade bed he saw in profile.

Chuck felt his mother touch his elbow and leave her hand there. "What are you looking at?" she said.

✚

The next day, Chuck walked around the block to the McDermotts' house. As he approached he saw that some of the grass of their lawn had been dug up; fist-sized divots covered the yard. When he got close he read the word *slut* carved into the black dirt under the McDermotts' lawn. The letters were deep, wide in some places and narrow in others, and were of different sizes as though more than one person had done the work.

Chuck walked through the yard and the rusted cast iron gate to the entryway, and pushed the doorbell. Mr. McDermott answered. He was a tall man with a full mustache. Chuck had seen him drive by the house on his way to work many times. Mr. McDermott had on a pair of tan slacks and a maroon robe that hung on him like a loose hide. He opened the door and looked at Chuck.

"We have to talk, Mr. McDermott," Chuck said.

Mr. McDermott nodded solemnly, as though he knew what Chuck was going to say, and turned to walk back into the house. From behind, Chuck noticed that Mr. McDermott limped as he walked. With his left hand, he reached around and held his right side, bracing his steps. "Do you want something to drink?" he said. "I've got milk and grapefruit juice."

"No. I'm here to talk to you about your wife."

They went into the family room. Mr. McDermott sat down on a low sofa and motioned for Chuck to sit in a green over-stuffed chair facing him.

"Shoot," Mr. McDermott said.

"Your wife," Chuck said. "It's your wife. She's been seducing my father underneath the acacia trees. Maybe you already know about it, I don't know, but my mother found out about it and it's going to destroy my parents' marriage. Something's got to be done. That's what I'm here to tell you. I'm here to tell you to do something about your wife."

Mr. McDermott stood up. He looked angry at first, turning around, glancing from side to side as if looking for something to break. His limp seemed to temporarily vanish in his rage. But when he turned back to Chuck he had calmed, and looked analytical, like a teacher Chuck had approached with a problem.

"Come here," he said, motioning for Chuck to follow. "Come with me."

He led them into the kitchen. Set up over the sink, a squat orange telescope looked out a screened window into the McDermotts' backyard. The telescope sat on a tripod of aluminum poles, one of which was jammed into the sink drain. Mr. McDermott walked to it and looked through the eyepiece, a cylinder the size of a toe that jutted out from the orange shaft. He adjusted some of the tripod dials and shifted one of the aluminum legs. "Okay," he said. He moved away from the telescope, careful not to disturb it. "Look through here."

Chuck walked to the sink and stooped to look through the eyepiece. He closed one eye and moved around until he saw a light, and stopped, centering it. He saw a large brown oval, on an angle, and a blurry circle inside of it. "That's 200X," Mr. McDermott said. "And it's upside down. The telescope turns it upside down." He walked around to Chuck's side and the view jiggled with his steps. Chuck tried to imagine what he saw right side up. It could have been a nipple. He reached up delicately and held the eyepiece with his thumb and forefinger, twisting in an attempt to focus. Nothing happened.

"I thought they just did it in the afternoons," Chuck said.

He waited for Mr. McDermott to say something. After a moment he heard, "That's not your father, Chuck. That's Russell Hall out there."

Chuck knew who Russell Hall was. He was the McDermotts' next-door neighbor. His son Tim had delivered newspapers all through high school and then gone to Purdue. Chuck looked up from the telescope and saw that it was not pointing at the acacias, but at two shoulder-high hedges growing between the McDermotts' yard and the Halls'. There was a small open gap in one of the hedges, near a pomegranate tree. "My wife's a troubled woman," Mr. McDermott said. "She's had a hard life. She's had some bad luck. She needs understanding."

Faintly, Chuck heard his father start playing his clarinet from the other side of the acacias.

"Did you see the lawn out front?" Mr. McDermott said.

"Yes."

"Know who did it?"

"No."

Mr. McDermott nodded. "Listen, my wife's a troubled woman and your father is taking advantage of that. He's the one you should be talking to. He's the one doing the damage here. You talk to him."

Before either of them said anything else, Mr. McDermott started coughing. It began subtly, as though he had something caught in his throat, but then huge bursts of air came from his mouth, as though he wanted to retch something up. He seemed unable to breathe, but looked surprisingly calm. Mr. McDermott heaved and hunched like a porcupine. He limped to the sink and looked over his shoulder and waved that he was fine. He turned back to the sink and spit and Chuck heard the saliva smack against the metal. Chuck let himself out, walked across the gouged lawn, and listened to Mr. McDermott's coughing until he was three houses away, where the sound was covered by the voices of two men loading a glass table into a long yellow moving van.

When he got home, Chuck walked straight through the house and out the sliding back door. The backyard was a neat and orderly place now. The grass was green with wide, healthy blades, the bushes and trees were free of caterpillars and aphids, and Chuck's father's tools, including the rake, the lawn mower, and the fertilizer spreader, leaned against the side of the house in an even line ordered by height.

Chuck walked out onto the grass. His father, still playing the clarinet, took the instrument away from his face when he saw his son approaching. Yellow light glistened off a strand of saliva that stretched between his lips and the wooden reed.

"What?" Chuck's father said.

"I know what you're doing out here," Chuck said. "I know what's going on. I've been watching you from upstairs." He turned and pointed up at the alcove window. "The first time — okay. The first time was not your fault. But you kept going back." He stopped, not knowing what more to say. He looked down at his father's feet. A long-legged bug climbed off one of his father's shoes and fell clumsily into the grass, flailing its body in circles. "What's wrong with you?" Chuck said.

"Hey, listen," his father said, "you don't know what goes on out here. You don't know what happens. It may not be what you think."

"Right."

"How would you know? What makes you think you know anything? If you knew anything you wouldn't be here right now, would you? You'd be in college. You'd have a job."

They stood there awkwardly for a moment. Chuck's father looked over his shoulder at the acacias, then back down at the clarinet. He fingered one of the keys repeatedly, testing to see if the cork was loose, and walked past Chuck into the house.

✛

Chuck locked himself in the guest room and called Sharon.

He wanted to give her an update. He still thought she might provide useful feedback. He dialed her number quickly and unconsciously. A male voice answered.

"Yeah?"

"Is Sharon there?"

There was pause and Chuck heard a breath. "This is Chuck, isn't it?"

"Yes," Chuck said.

"Why don't you leave Sharon alone? She hates your guts. She doesn't want to know you anymore."

"That's not true. Sharon does not hate my guts."

"Listen," the voice said. "You know what I'm going to do if you keep calling here? I'm going to kill you."

○

That night, a lantern lit up in Mrs. McDermott's cave. Orange light streamed in thin rays through open spaces between the small cupped leaves. The yard was eerily lit. Chuck and his parents stood at the sliding glass door looking out at the strange glow.

"Damnedest thing," Chuck's father said. "Maybe I should go out there."

Chuck looked at his parents' images reflecting off the door. They were ghostly, ringed with orange light, barely there.

"I don't think so," Chuck's mother said. "This isn't any of our business." She dragged on a cigarette and blew smoke into the glass. "This really doesn't have one thing to do with us."

"Still, I think I should go out and at least see what's going on. Maybe there's trouble."

"I don't think you need to do that."

"I do. You never know."

Chuck's father slid aside the glass door, stepped out, and closed the door behind him. When it shut, Chuck's mother said, "Can you believe that? After what I just said?"

She switched off a lamp so they could see out. Chuck's father glanced back and then headed across the grass toward the acacias. The orange light made a silhouette of him. Chuck and his mother watched silently for the first few steps.

"I'm really going to divorce him," Chuck's mother said. "You're my witness, Chuck. Before it was just talk. Now, I'm really serious about this."

Chuck's father made it to the hole and crawled in, disturbing the light that shone out to the house. After a moment, the lantern dimmed and went out. Chuck watched for a while longer, then stepped away and went into the kitchen. Ten minutes later, when his father came back in, Chuck and his mother sat together at the counter. They turned when they heard the door and watched him walk across the room to the sink. The knees of his pants had mud stains the size of pancakes.

He washed his hands and said, "That was Karen McDermott out there. You wouldn't believe it. She's got a little hole cut out in those bushes."

"Really?" Chuck's mother said.

"Yeah. That lantern was hanging from a broken branch. I thought it might fall so I turned it out."

"What the hell's she doing out there?"

Chuck's father took a glass from an overhead cabinet and filled it with water from the tap. "I don't know," he said. "She kept saying her husband was gone. 'Raymond is gone. Raymond is gone.' She was inconsolable, so I came back in." He drank the water quickly, letting drops of it seep around the corners of his mouth.

"Maybe he left her," Chuck's mother said. Her eyes grew to queer eggs and her face went blood-red. It was the kind of look that let Chuck imagine her outside at night, her breath making vapor, working with a hoe to cut hateful words into a neighbor's yard. "That's happening a lot. I hear Linda Hall is thinking about giving Russell his walking papers."

"Maybe," Chuck's father said. Their eyes met and they stared at each other.

"Maybe he died," Chuck said. "Maybe he's dead in the house somewhere and she's too whacked out to do anything about it."

Out the kitchen window Chuck saw a match strike in Mrs. McDermott's cave, and the lantern light back up. When Mrs. McDermott moved or hit a tree branch, the light poked out different holes, causing the whole wall to twinkle. Chuck's parents stared at each other for a long while, until at last his mother said, in a quiet voice, "We know, Rob. Me and Chuck, we know everything."

Chuck called Sharon from the guest room. He lay back on

the bare mattress and listened to his parents' voices filtered through the house as he dialed. When Sharon answered, he wasn't ready for it.

"Hello, Sharon," he said. "What's going on?"

"I got into Berkeley," she said. She said it like she had just slit open the letter, or like she was rubbing it in. "Why are you calling me?"

"Is Steve there?"

"No."

"I need to talk to you. My parents are having trouble. They're downstairs arguing right now. I think they're thinking about divorce. It's out of hand. I thought you might be able to steer me in the right direction. I don't know what I'd do if they got divorced."

"I thought you said you wished they would get divorced," Sharon said.

"When did I say that?"

"One time."

"I never said that."

"Yes, you did. A long time ago."

"Why would I say that?" Chuck said. "Okay, maybe I did say it. Everybody says that at some point. But just because I said it doesn't mean I meant it. These are my parents."

"Hey, listen, Chuck," Sharon said, "while you're on the phone I think I ought to tell you something."

"What?" He sat up on the bare mattress. The tips of his toes rubbed against the carpet.

"It's about your dad. The truth of it is, Chuck, we slept together a couple times."

"You're lying."

"No, it's the truth. It was that year you were in the band. I'd come over while you were at practice. No one'd be home." She paused and Chuck sat listening. He looked down at the mattress.

Sharon was chewing gum. "You probably hate me now, huh, Chuck?" she said. "You probably think I'm a whore. Don't you hate me now?"

Early the next morning, Chuck's father set his hand on Chuck's hip and shook him awake. "What are you doing here?" he said.

They were in the guest room. Chuck had fallen asleep listening to his parents' voices. He rubbed his eyes and shrugged.

"Listen," his father said, whispering. "I've got news. I'm leaving tonight. I'm going away with Karen—with Mrs. McDermott."

"You're leaving?"

"Yes. I'm here to say good-bye to my only son. I want you to know that I don't hold it against you that you gave me away to your mother. You didn't know what you were doing. I can sympathize with that."

"You can't leave. You can't go with her."

"Why not?"

"Mrs. McDermott is a troubled woman," Chuck said. "She's had bad luck. You're taking advantage of her."

"Who are you?" his father said. "Mr. Know-it-all? That woman does things for me. Listen, you don't know what I'm talking about, do you? You have no comprehension at all of what I'm talking about. I love her. I love this woman." He pointed out the alcove window, through which they could see the early glow of the sky.

Chuck's father stood and looked at his watch. "Look, I have to finish packing. I have a few things to collect yet. I want to be out of here by five-thirty. I'll be back in a little bit when I'm ready to take off. Stay here, okay?"

He left the room. Chuck got up and went downstairs. The digital clock in the kitchen said 5:19. Outside, the sky was slowly lighting up, mixing with the electric light on the back porch. In the dimness the acacias looked solid as stone; Mrs. McDermott's cave was dark. Chuck heard his father's footsteps upstairs going from room to room. After a little while he heard his mother's as well, softer, the pace quicker, following his father's around.

Chuck opened the sliding glass door. He had on a pair of shorts and a T-shirt. The air that rushed into the room was refreshing at first, then cold. He stepped out onto the concrete path that led around the house, and then onto the grass, wet with dew. The soft blades stuck in between his toes and his feet dripped water in between his steps. As he approached the line of acacias he looked for the small flower buds. They would be white flowers soon, with long pink pistils, and from the house the acacias would look streaked like marble, ribbed with white veins.

He walked to Mrs. McDermott's cave. The entrance was black. He did a deep knee bend on the grass but could not see in. He pried back a branch and crawled in the hole. A thorn scraped along his shoulder, pulling at his shirt. He could see nothing. He advanced to where he guessed the center of the cave was and pivoted on the balls of his hands to sit down. He set his elbows on his knees and cupped his hands together for warmth. He sat there for a short while, letting the water that had accumulated on the acacia leaves drip down on his hair from above. He rubbed his feet to dry them.

Then he heard a sound that was not him. It was inside the cave, a breath, a throaty animal noise. He opened his eyes wider to see better, but it didn't help. A hand touched his thigh, and moved away quickly. Its heat and the fingernails he felt gave him shivers, and then goosebumps. Water dripped all around him. He heard a voice say, "Hello. Hi." It was a soft voice, not distinctly male or female, and Chuck could not discern exactly where it was coming from. He listened for a moment, and then slowly crawled out of the cave.

He stood up in the grass. In the house, he saw a light go on in the alcove of the guest room. After a second, a shadowy figure rose into view. It stopped at the window, looking down. Chuck stayed where he was. He couldn't tell if the figure was his mother, close to the glass, watching this spot as she frequently had, or his father, a few steps back, shocked and frozen in place.

The voice spoke again, behind Chuck. "Hello," it said. "Hi there. Come here." Chuck's hands shook and bounced off his thighs. He made fists and locked his elbows. He picked up one foot and then the other; they were numb with mud and wet and cold. He turned back to the acacia trees, kneeled slowly and shut his eyes, and readied himself to face whatever waited in the shady recess of the cave.

THE HOSPITAL FOR BAD POETS

In all things, however, you act too familiarly with the spirit, and you have often made wisdom into a poorhouse and a hospital for bad poets.

—Nietzsche

I was discovered on the floor of my room some two months after I'd begun to write poetry. It was the maid who found me, silly woman, deaf as a nail—she dialed emergency and sputtered her nonsense until they traced the call. It was luck, they said, that there was a crew nearby who knew how to handle a case like mine.

"Hey, bub!" the first of the emergency crew said, testing my shoulder with a finger. "Can you hear me?"

I groaned humble acknowledgment.

"I'm Mike. This is Bob. We're with the ambulance. Mind if we check you out?"

They were blue-collar men in manner despite the massive training. Mike was just a bud, scarcely emerged from his school years, while Bob's mustache showed his seasoning. They might have been father and son.

Before I could respond, Bob placed a latex palm on Mike's shoulder, pressing down gently.

"What'd we forget?"

Mike looked over the equipment they'd humped to my walk-up, then figured it. "Oh, shoot. Is he alone?"

"He *appears* alone, but it's still the first thing you should ask yourself."

"Right." Mike nodded and turned back to me. "Are you alone?"

"Well, I was writing, so of course I was alone. But there is my maid."

She was standing just beside us, smiling as I nodded to her. I could compose in her presence precisely because the poor woman couldn't make out whatever I might utter whilst before the keyboard.

"One poet on the scene," Mike said.

"Good," Bob said. "And what do we know about him so far?"

"He can talk. He has an airway. If you don't have an airway, you don't have a poet."

"Bingo," Bob said. "Proceed."

Mike leaned down to where I lay supine. "Who are you? What happened here today? Who is the president of the United States? Do you know roughly what time it is?"

"Shhh," Bob said, patting the boy's back. "Let him answer."

I came to the conclusion that Mike was a newcomer, a trainee—like me—studying under the tutelage of an old hand, a mentor. I took it as a good sign that Bob didn't feel a need to step in and get me quickly to the truck.

I told them my name. I was still an unknown. I knew the president, swine that he is, and I knew it was afternoon because that's when the muse arrives. But I had no recollection of how I'd gotten onto the floor or whether I'd been there a minute or an hour.

"Oriented times three," Mike said, scribbling the conclusion on a pad.

"What does that mean?" I said.

"It means you got three out of four," Bob said. "Great for Barry Bonds. And not bad for a poet, either."

"Chief complaint," Mike said.

"What?"

"What seems to be bothering you?"

This I did not know. No part of me hurt, exactly, but nor can I say that I felt completely well. It seemed best to defer to the evidence at hand—surely, the strain of work had caused me to convulse and perhaps I had struck my head on the way down—but how could I describe this to my nurses? The words did not come. Mike and Bob adopted an identical look of professional concern, the younger man imitating his elder half a beat slow.

"What are our pertinent negatives?" Bob said.

"No blood. Poet reports no pain, but that can be deceiving. No obvious deformities. No suicidal ideations, which might be expected given the nature of the call."

"Good," Bob said. "How about signs? The entire scene may be filled with clues."

Mike scanned my room until Bob nodded him to my typewriter. My latest dangled from the spool like a sheet of half-rolled dough. The boy ripped the page free to examine it. "Is this the last thing you were working on?"

"It's not finished," I said. "Obviously."

"Notice," Bob said, "that a lot of the time poets aren't 100 percent cooperative even when the goal is to help them. God knows why."

But the boy wasn't listening. His eyes rode the toppled columns of my lines.

"This is awful," Mike said.

I groaned and my head hit the floor, perhaps for the second time.

"Watch that C-spine, Mike!" Bob said. "You can't be held liable for disliking the work of a bad poet, but you are responsible for insufficient care. Granted, we're not dealing with the penetrating trauma of a slam poet or gangsta rapper here, but even a standard verse emergency runs circles around your typical diabetic episode. This is a poet! And poets can go south fast. Look the wrong way and even Wordsworth will take the big six-foot dirt nap. Poets have feelings up the ass."

"Sorry," Mike said, and he eased down to a crouch and placed a palm on either side of my head to steady it.

"We're at the end of our initial assessment," Bob said. "Are we stay and play, or are we load and go?"

"No frank hemorrhaging. Poet appears perfused. He looks disappointed, but that's hardly worth risking red lights and siren." Mike bit his lip. "Stay and play?"

Bob nodded proudly.

Mike looked down at me, reading my inverted expression, and continued his assessment. "What's your favorite form?"

"The sonnet."

"When was the last time you employed iambic pentameter?"

"In a poem? Forget it, I don't know."

"How do you know when a poem is over?"

"A poem is never over. You abandon it." I propped myself up on my elbows and looked down at my legs. I could feel my toes. "You know, I'm beginning to feel a little better. Maybe I just needed an audience to—"

"Ho there, cowboy!" Bob said, lunging forward to steady my shoulders. "Think about what you're doing. You could have writer's block. You might even have a clot. Stand up and you're talking ischemic stroke. You could have an aneurysm in your language center. It goes pop, you'll never even *think* verse again." He lodged his hands against his hips, decisively. "We've got to take you to the hospital for bad poets."

"No," I said. "God, no."

"Don't be embarrassed. Some of our greatest poets have been hospitalized, often against their will. Lowell, Plath, Pound, Berryman, Carruth, Sexton, Roethke, Hesse, Jarrell, Hecht, Schwarz, Williams. The pain isn't necessary, my friend. They're there to help."

It was getting a little harder to breathe. I nodded implied consent.

"Okay, Mike. What does everyone get?"

"Oxygen."

"Right. Make it six liters by nasal cannula. And what does every poet get?"

"Rilk-ee."

"Rilk-*uh*, Mike. They all get Rilk-uh."

Mike handed me a book. It was *Duino Elegies*. "Read," he told me.

They put me on the sheeted cart to steer me to the ambulance. My maid held the door and waved as we rolled away.

✚

At the hospital for bad poets I was labeled an emergent case. But what was emerging? Doctors and nurses frenzied about me, and they called in a scholar to sit by my head and whisper in my ear. He was a little man in black, he had no callus on his finger, and he murmured from a tiny copy of *The Sacred Wood,* bound in leather panels dyed green.

I was diagnosed with chronic acuteness.

My friends Mike and Bob chatted with my doctor, a youngish man named Krupp. He wore a slick Vandyke.

"Third poet we had tonight," Dr. Krupp said. "What is this, a full moon?"

"They always come in threes," a nurse said, rushing past with a bag of syringes.

"No shit." Krupp sauntered my way, snapping his plastic into place. "How are you doing, pal? Is that Rilk-ee helping you any? Let me know if you're having any pain. We don't like pain. Pain we can do something about."

"Every good poem betrays someone," I said. "Pain is the spring of beauty."

"Have it your way. But don't worry, we'll have you back in front of the ol' word processor as soon as we rule out carpal tunnel."

"I write longhand."

"Sure you do, pal, sure you do," Dr. Krupp said. "Now what seems to be the problem today? What's the last thing you remember? How's your thyroid? How's your medulla oblongata?" Krupp looked over his shoulder and screamed. "What are the vitals on this guy? Where's the frigging 12-lead? Call the photoshop, tell them to plug in the Cat."

"But, doctor," said a nurse, "the Cat costs ten thousand dollars a pop!"

"You think I don't know that?"

"He doesn't have any insurance. Few poets do."

Dr. Krupp slapped his hand across a cabinet to atomize his fury. The whole wall shook. "Damn this bureaucracy, damn its dollars and bottom lines. Do you want to look the world in the face when you've lost, possibly, another Byron, a Whitman, a Baudelaire? Where would we be without poets? To wit: 'The poet takes everything good from life and puts it into his work. Thus, his life is bad but his poetry is good.'" Krupp swung around on his heels and pointed a finger at me. "Guess the quote."

"Nietzsche?" I groaned.

"Tolstoy," sighed the nurse.

Dr. Krupp frowned. "Well, I suppose you're here for a reason, after all." To the nurse: "We have a responsibility to this man, nurse. He may be a bad poet, but please call the photoshop, anyway, and ask them nicely to turn on their precious machine."

I answered Dr. Krupp's questions as best I could. My thyroid felt fine as far as I could tell, and though *medulla oblongata* was a phrase ripe with poetic potential I admitted that I hadn't known I had one. The last thing I remembered, now that I thought about it, was the final line I had intoned onto my ancient Smith Corona. The poem was a half-finished villanelle about a tribe in New Guinea I'd spent a week researching. I loved their land, their warrior way. When someone died in tribal warfare, the women chopped the top knuckle off a finger. My line was about the stubs that formed when the fingers healed. But before I could muster the strength to rise for a recitation, Mike stepped forward with the poem itself. He and Bob had stuck around. If I survived until admission it might mean a commendation for them, maybe a little press coverage.

Dr. Krupp snatched the poem away and his eyes gobbled up its heathen panorama. "This sucks," he said.

"I'm a beginner," I said. "The world of poetry is itself fractured and ill. Who's to say what's good and what's bad? It's the language poets' fault, really."

"Your EKG will read more interesting than this," Krupp said. "Can you sit up? I need to hear your breath sounds."

The plastic curtain strung all around us suddenly parted to reveal a dozen young medical students with bright white coats and identical stethoscopes laid across their shoulders like stoles. They crowded in with ministeps.

"We're a teaching hospital," Dr. Krupp said. "These are some of our students. With your permission they'll simply observe." He didn't wait for an answer, unwrapping his own stethoscope, an electronic-assist model, and setting the earpieces in place. He tapped the diaphragm once to test it. "Now you won't see it in *JAMA* or the *New England*

Journal of Medicine," he told the class, "but the latest coming out of literary circles is something called 'intimacy theory.' The basic idea is that poets control readers' breath sounds. They breathe together. The relationship between poet and reader is closer to the relationship between conductor and musician than between conductor and audience. Who reads poetry? Anyone?"

It took a moment for the students to work out the grammar of the questioning.

"Poets read poets, doctor," said an intern.

"Yes. Now we could simply lament this and complain that our sanitized world has turned our main streets into a sterile vacuum of high-tech malls, that culture is what we scrape from the back of the poet's throat and send to the lab for tests, but this, I'm afraid, would miss the subtler point. Poets require a different sort of triage. Think of ventilating a patient. You breathe for them. You force high flow O_2 into their lungs to displace the carbon dioxide that can make them hyperacidic. Now poetry is—and this is my personal theory, you won't find it in any book—poetry is the equivalent of ventilation. Poets breathe for one another, they breathe for all of us. Poets blow a sense of beauty and morality into a world stuck on the exhale. Without them we would rocket off to spiritual vacuity like a balloon."

To this point, Krupp had played absently with the head of his stethoscope, dangling it like a baited hook. Now he looked down and its presence shook him from reverie. He turned back to me.

"Very well. Breath sounds. Remove your shirt."

He helped me off with my garment, and the chill of the diaphragm drained my warmth.

"Deep breath and hold," Dr. Krupp said.

I inhaled until my lungs felt tight.

"Now quote," he said.

I said:

"Sorry hospital echoing with sighs
Adorned by one enormous crucifix,
Where tearful prayers rise from excrement
And a sudden ray of winter sunlight falls."

Dr. Krupp moved the stethoscope down my back and placed a palm on my chest. He pressed. "Again," he said.

"Now comes the time when invalids grow worse
And darkness takes them by the throat; they end
Their fate in the usual way, and all their sighs
Turn hospitals into a cave of winds."

Another spot, higher now. "No repeating," Krupp said.

"The wounded surgeon plies the steel
That questions the distempered part;
Beneath the bleeding hands we feel
The sharp compassion of the healer's art
Resolving the enigma of the fever chart."

"And once more," Krupp said.

"All of the sick who endure disease's course
In Val de Chiana's hospital from July
All through September, and all the sufferers
In Maremma and Sardinia, to lie
All in one ditch together, so was this place."

"Good," Dr. Krupp said. To the class: "Opinions?"

A young man raised a ballpoint pen. "Poet's choices appear to indicate depression and possible S.I. Contact psych for social worker intervention."

Krupp gestured ambivalence. "There's nothing in the run report to indicate such. Remember, not all poetry is happy limericks about men from Nantucket. Even a random sampling of poets reveals elevated levels of moodiness and irascibility. But still, perhaps a wise precaution." He nodded to a nurse, who took a note. "Anyone else?"

A young woman had obtained the copy of my unfinished villanelle; I had watched her read it while Krupp sermonized— breath held. Now she spoke without looking away. "Poet's voice is strained. Prolonged bed rest without discourse is indicated. As well, poet's thinking is nonabstract and narrative-centric. A long-term prescription for law school appears warranted."

Krupp grimaced and hissed. "Gosh, I hate to lose one just because of a single collapse. He's only been at this a couple of months, you'll recall. Now that could mean a weak constitution, yes, but it could also signal dedication and discipline. Let's not condemn him just yet. Let's admit him for a week, keep him under observation, post a guard at his door, and—"

A nurse bounded toward us, braking at Krupp's elbow. "Doctor! The poet in five! He's about to code!"

The interns couldn't hide their excitement, but Dr. Krupp sagged on his feet. "Not another one!" he cried. "If every poet codes, who will understand them? Poetry is hard enough already. Who has time to unriddle the ordinary?" He shook his head. "We're not miracle workers. We can't resuscitate them all."

"Doctor, we must hurry."

Krupp looked at me once more, with a kind of disgust. Then he shook it off to swish away to a case more emergent than my own. His interns followed him like a royal train, and Mike and Bob followed along as well, the two of them exchanging a high five on the news that I would be admitted to the hospital for bad poets.

When they were gone, I saw my maid standing amidst the sterile white of the room. She had followed the ambulance, the dear woman. She approached my bed. We exchanged no words at all, and she held my hand.

THE FIRE

Ned was driving home from work when the ash began to fall. The odd flakes, tossed in the wind rush of moving cars, described an insistent pain beating time inside his head. The radio had warned that the fire had changed directions, but still his body reacted as though to a surprise. The ash fell like a black snow. Ned tried to ignore it and the pain both, concentrating on the thickened traffic. He eased up on the accelerator, raised the automatic windows, and drifted into a premature dusk.

He arrived home in twenty minutes. Elise and the children had gathered in the front yard, ash catching in their hair and lashes. The boy, nine, and the girl, six, ran circles on the small lawn. They hadn't ever seen snow, so this was exciting.

Ned parked and walked across the drive. Elise wore a white apron. She was still a pretty woman, with cheekbones curving like knives to points near her ears. The ash in her hair made her look gray and aged.

He gestured at the downpour. "Amazing."

"I guess so," Elise said, her attention fixed on the boy and girl.

"It means it's coming our way now."

She looked at him out the crease of her eye. "You'll scare the children."

The ash began to gather by the curb. Up the street, Ned's neighbors stood in their yards, marveling. Some had gathered in groups. Ned stared at the people who lived and slept near him, recognizing just a few here and there, and wondered why it was only disaster that jarred them from their private spaces. By then, the sky was a dark ceiling a hundred feet up. The children giggled and tried to catch falling flakes on their hands.

The sweet smell of burning chaparral had been in the air since the fire started, but as tissue-thin mounds of ash formed near Ned's feet, he caught the scent of another fire, something close. He made his body stiff as wood.

"What?" Elise said.

It felt good to have her look at him. "Something's burning."

She tilted her head back and inhaled. "That's my meat," she said, and jogged into the house, wiping ashy hands on her apron.

Ned followed her inside and climbed the stairs to the bedroom.

The fire was coming in behind them, from the northeast. Ned retrieved a meter-long telescope from a closet and carried it out the door that connected the bedroom to the sun deck. The house sat on the edge of the subdivision. Just behind the backyard fence the land pitched, the hillside dropping thirty feet at a forty-degree grade, making an incidental streambed at the bottom. From there, the land descended gradually for more than ten miles, a bumpy granite-spackled plain that ended at the horizon's roller-coaster of brown hills. Ned looked into the dark plume rising from the plain, seven miles off. The ash feathered all around him as he unfolded the telescope's aluminum tripod. He aimed with the sighting scope that rode sidecar to the main shaft, then switched to the main scope and focused.

The fire was a huge, glistening orange wall. It swept across the patches of chamise and manzanita, flames lapping at the air like waves on a lakeshore. Below, tiny men dressed in gas masks and yellow protective gear fought back with Weed Eaters and small bulldozers. White streams of water arced into the blaze and came out as steam. Ned's view waved like a mirage in the fire's heat. His headache spiked, and he looked up from the eyepiece to steady himself. He dug his fingers into his temples and told himself it was stress. Stress.

He switched to a higher power and scanned again until he found several firefighters attempting to cut a break along an erosion gully. They used chain saws to eat away at yucca, and one had a tool whose metal head was a pick at one end and an ax at the other. They failed to notice bright sparks tumbling over their heads in the breeze. Spots of flame sprouted behind them, and they scattered like dizzy yellow ants.

Ned returned the telescope to the closet. He'd bought the thing intending to share it with his son, but the boy had quickly lost interest. Ned had used the scope to watch the fire on several occasions, once viewing a huge silver B-17 as it strafed the fire with a torrent of red chemicals.

He walked to the kitchen, where the fluorescent light was cool and clean. Elise was still cooking dinner. He stepped behind her as she chopped potatoes at the sink and set his hands gently on her waist. She was warm through her blue jeans.

"Don't," she said. "Please, stop."

Ned paused, but retreated to the counter. Her words rang like chimes, and his imagination corrected the jumble: *please, don't stop.* Years before, as a condition to marriage, Elise had suggested a pact: she would raise the children for their first decade if Ned would agree to the same for the next. An idealistic law student at the time, Ned had agreed, and the pact disappeared. He landed a partner-track position at a bankruptcy firm. Then, on the ten-year anniversary of the pact, Elise announced that she had been taking pottery classes for some time and wanted to open a shop to sell jugs and bowls. Ned was shocked that she had hidden this from him. He tried to take her proposal seriously, but her faith in success was ridiculous. He should give up the job that had provided them with the station of their lives before she had so much as drafted a business plan?

He made a counter offer: he would take a year's hiatus from the firm and if by the end of that time she wasn't in the black, he would return and take the vows of partner. Elise claimed breach of contract. "We had a deal," she said. She threatened to leave if he didn't quit the firm in six months.

Elise lit the stove and unwrapped a package of meat. Ned stared at the burner, the circle of curly blue flames. They were steady, tame. A minute passed before Elise took a stab at civility.

"I burned the last one. We all went outside when the ash started." She held up the porous slab of red meat. "That's what you smelled."

"I figured."

Glancing up, she said, "Look at you."

Ned looked at himself in the glass door of the oven. He was covered with ash, appeared in the tinted glass as he might look in thirty years.

She gestured at the ceiling. "Any change?"

"No. What's the news say?"

"'No one knows when the fire will be under control.'"

"Wonderful."

"What's that mean exactly? To have it 'under control'?"

"I don't know," Ned said.

Out the kitchen window, the streetlights came on weak and pale. The ash grew thicker. Elise opened her mouth as if to speak again, but changed her mind.

Ned leaned toward her. "What were you going to say?"

"Nothing."

He waited for her to change her mind. He tried to brush some of the ash flakes off his jacket sleeve, but they only smeared into the fabric.

✛

The wind shifted four hours later. The fire headed east and the ash flew off, leaving behind a thin charcoal dust. In the morning, Ned examined the burn scar through the telescope. It spread across the plain like a giant black circus ring. White smoke rose from shriveled scrub, and rock outcroppings were dark with heavy soot.

He went out front to brush the ash from the driveway. The sky was blue again. The ash had sprinkled roofs, patios, trees, the street. Some of Ned's neighbors had the same idea he had. A woman used a push broom to coax the ash into her lawn. A man used a Port-a-vac to suck the stuff up. Ned fashioned an awkward scoop from a cardboard box. He dug a weightless load from a heap near the front door, only to find himself at a loss for how to dispose of it. His next-door neighbor, a man named Stillwell, popped out from behind the tall hedge that separated their yards.

"Good thing it didn't rain," Stillwell said. "Stuff would have got right into our paint."

Ned glanced at the upper story of his home. "Lucky."

Stillwell was a lanky man; he wore thick-rimmed glasses. Ned had never spoken to him, and knew his name only because it was printed on his mailbox.

"Saw you up on your deck last night," Stillwell said. "Get a good look?"

"It's out of control," Ned said. "It's an inferno."

Stillwell stepped up onto the lawn, a cloud of ash lofting featherlike behind him. "Under proper wind and fuel conditions," he said, "the Southern California biota is notorious for high fireline intensity." He smirked and admitted, "I've been doing some reading."

"Ah." Ned looked down at his cardboard spade. His headache had eased when the fire turned.

"We're in what's known as a fire-climax community," Stillwell said. "The problem is, we burn as well as the scrubland. It has yucca and oak, we've got palm trees and wood shingles. There is no accepted treatment for the suburb-chaparral ecotone. The fire," he said, "doesn't know the difference."

"Fire climax," Ned said.

Stillwell smiled. "Sounds like something you might want to try, doesn't it?" He chuckled and scratched the back of his neck. Ned caught a glimmer of something behind the man's glasses. The rest of his face moved with his laughter, but his eyes floated steadily behind the lenses like animals preserved in formaldehyde.

"Use bags," Stillwell said, motioning to the ash falling from Ned's plank. "Plastic garbage bags. Pumice will get it off your hands."

"Thanks," Ned said.

Stillwell waved and disappeared back behind the hedge.

Ned didn't have bags, so he used a plastic trash bin from the garage. The ash came up easily. It took him an hour to clear the driveway and cars. When he went inside, he tracked ash across the beige carpet in the living room. Elise, appearing in the kitchen doorway, said, "Stop."

Ned froze and realized what he'd done. He turned at the hip and looked back at the splotchy footsteps. Elise jogged over and kneeled next to one of them.

"It'll come out," he said.

"Take off your shoes," Elise said.

He obeyed. The bottoms of his shoes were dark as asphalt. He removed his socks as well and found that the ash had coated his legs.

Elise began work on the stains with a damp rag. "Warm water and a sponge. Hurry."

Ned fetched these things, plus a liquid hand cleaner that had pumice in it. Elise set the plastic bottle aside and worked silently. She didn't ask anything more of him, so he went into the family room and sank into the sofa. He returned the gray stare of the television for a while, then picked up the message pad and pen from beside the telephone. He wrote on the paper:

ELISE

ELITE

DELETE

He studied the progression for a moment and tore off the top sheet. As an afterthought, he tore off the next few sheets and crumpled these as well, in case the point of the pen had pressed images into them.

He glanced at the phone. An information service had been set up for the owners of endangered homes. The hotline furnished reports on incident status and made fire behavior predictions. The fire was moving away from them now. Ned called anyway.

The phone rang twice, and a woman answered. "Firewatch." Her voice was young but exhausted, her breathing a pant.

"What's the fire's location now?" Ned said.

"The main conflagration just spotted across highway 54. It's continuing east at a hundred feet per minute," the young woman said. "Two new blazes have ignited along I5, but are 90 percent contained. N.W.S. reports have the prevailing winds holding until at least tomorrow."

"Good."

"Good for you, bad for other people," the young woman said.

Ned wanted to stay on the line. The voice was reassuring. He tried to picture her, and the face he imagined cooled his headache, wound it into a ball. "Have there been any fatalities?"

Her breathing stopped. "This hotline is for civilian use only. If you're a reporter, I can have you fined."

"No, no," Ned said. "I live close to it. I was just wondering. I've got kids."

She paused. "Six."

"Any children?"

"Two."

"Christ."

"How close are you?"

"Close," he said.

"I have to go," the young woman said. "My lights are blinking."

Ned puttered around the house for the rest of the day. He had decided not to go to work the night before, when scrolling messages on the television announced school closings. He went out back and stood in the yard. An hour passed in which the only movement he saw was a shuffle in the boughs of a eucalyptus tree. The ash came out of the carpet, but it took Elise a couple of hours. Ned felt guilty for letting her do the work alone. He made lunch for the children, and then dinner as well. By nightfall, he was unaccountably tired. He watched half a sitcom and went upstairs.

He took out the telescope and scanned the hills through the sliding glass door. All darkness. After a time, he opened the door and stepped out onto the deck. The air was chilly. He walked the deck's length trying to distinguish the billows of dark smoke from the blackness of space along the eastern horizon. He heard voices from Stillwell's house. Grayish shadows passed behind a lit window. He could not make out what the voices were saying, but he could hear the angry emotion of the language. The voices took turns for a while, trading bitter speeches, then went at it together, a mess of words. They sputtered at last and fell into silence.

Above and to the north, the moon cut a sharp crescent and glowed a mustardy brown from the smoke in the air. Ned's eyes fell to the lawn. He leaned over the rail, tracking to the end of the grass and over the backyard fence to that more severe drop. The land his house stood on was fill—dirt trucked here to give him a view. He felt dizzy. His headache shifted in his skull like a peanut in its shell, and he set his hand on the rail for balance. When he recovered, he saw Elise behind him.

"What's wrong?" she said.

He hoped she was referring to the Stillwells' argument. But they were quiet. "I'm not sure."

She took him by the arm and led him to the bed.

A local television station holding a marathon vigil reported on the turns the blaze made over the next forty-eight hours.

Coddled by Santa Ana conditions—foehn winds spilling out of the Great Basin—the fire swerved first to the northeast, destroying two mobile homes and an abandoned warehouse on Highway 210. During the night it crept down a westward slope, doubling back behind where it originally started, then rushing upslope in the morning and splitting into multiple heads along a drainage canal. That afternoon, a news helicopter filmed four firefighters as they were caught in a flashover of volatilized gases, and two more were lost when burning mine-shaft timbers buckled beneath their feet. At dusk, the spots of fire merged into a series of runs, breaching the fire line into a heavy fuel of scrub oak, redoubling in strength. Spreading at three hundred feet per minute, the fire formed an ellipse for most of the following day, and at three o'clock, the whole thing slid finally to the southeast, back toward Ned's house.

At four o'clock, a white minivan pulled up beside Ned's mailbox. Six men climbed out, wearing ties and hard hats, each carrying a clipboard. They spread out in six directions. Ned opened his front door when one of them approached.

"We're evacuating the area," the man said. He stopped ten feet off.

"When will it be here?" Ned said.

The man checked his watch. "Hard to tell. Conditions keep changing. It could veer off at any minute. Sometime tonight, I'd guess. Assuming we don't put it out by then, of course."

Ned had watched the fire from the deck for several hours. There was no one between himself and the blaze. His headache had reacted strangely to the fire's approach, folding in on itself to a single intense point. "I've been watching with my telescope. Where are all the firemen?"

The man grinned congenially. "Oh, they're there, don't worry. Be out by five." He touched the plastic brim of his hard hat.

The fire was still six miles out, but moved now at an easy jog. Gaining temperature over the Mojave and speed in the mountains east of Los Angeles, the warm gusts of the Santa Ana carried the stream of ash over Ned's house and beyond. Elise packed their valuables, allowing the children a small box for toys. Ned worked on clothing and toiletries. As he stuffed tiny jeans and underwear into a duffel bag in his son's room, Ned saw Stillwell out the window, packing a car in his driveway. Stillwell arranged suitcases in the trunk as his wife nestled their youngest into a baby seat. Ned counted four children altogether, the other three standing quietly on the lawn. When the car was ready, Stillwell's wife produced a set of keys and climbed into the driver's seat. The children piled in back. Stillwell remained by the hood, one hand casually in his pocket. His wife started the car and lurched into the street. Stillwell watched until they disappeared and then went inside.

Ned dropped the duffel and hurried downstairs. He found Elise beside a window, holding a butter knife from their wedding silver. She had witnessed the same scene he had seen.

"You're staying," she said.

"Yes."

"I knew it! Goddammit!" She moved to the dining room table, where the rest of the wedding silver was laid out. She looked at him, scoffed, and wrapped the knife in a dust rag. Ned went upstairs and finished packing for the children. When he came back down, Elise was on the edge of the living-room sofa, holding a decorative crystal plate in her lap. He took her in his arms, but she only stared at the floor.

Ned watched from the living room as his neighbors departed, packed cars rolling past the window. Evacuation centers had been set up at community clubs and senior-citizen centers, but Elise checked into a motel with the children. Ned heard television laughter in the background when she called from the room.

When the traffic eased, he went upstairs and looked at the fire through the telescope. It was four miles away by then, close enough to see with the naked eye. The flames fluttered in the coming twilight, the silent surf of a distant beach. There was nothing in the way of trucks or men.

At six o'clock, Stillwell came to the door. He wore a flannel shirt and work pants. Even behind his glasses, his look now was of something released. A station wagon idled in the driveway.

"There's no one out there," Ned said. "There's no firemen."

"I know," Stillwell said. "Want to go for a ride?"

Ned left the house open. Stillwell peeled into the street and steered them wildly through the residential maze, speeding through blind intersections, hopping curbs, the fire-hot wind rushing in the open windows. The subdivision was dim and deserted. A few families had left their sprinklers on, and others had wet their roofs. Ned sat forward in his seat and watched the houses flash by, completely alert for the first time since the fire started. His headache was gone. He closed his eyes and let the hot air rush into his mouth, clogging the cavity the pain left behind.

After a mile, Stillwell dug into his shirt pocket and produced a small white tablet. He cupped it in his palm to display it, and spoke over the wind. "Some Native American groups still use hallucinogens in their religious practices. Peyote, mainly, but others as well. Many of the rituals utilize fire and heat. The word *peyote* comes from the Aztecs, *Nahautal peyotl*. It means caterpillar." He held the small pill out to Ned. "Take this."

Ned pinched it, examined it. "What is it?"

"Just take it."

He popped it in his mouth and swallowed.

Stillwell swerved into a cul-de-sac, jerking the station wagon to a halt in the middle of the asphalt circle. He set the emergency brake but left the car running. He got out and dashed to the nearest house, hurdling a waist-high fence around the side. Ned watched as though he were at a drive-in, the world already beginning to flatten before him. Stillwell stayed out of sight for an interminable period, and in that desperate time everything Ned saw slackened and began to waver. When Stillwell reappeared he was carrying two garden hoses, one draped over each shoulder. He ran to the back of the car and dumped the green lengths through the rear window.

"You going to help?" he said, and ran off to another house.

Ned jumped out of the car and flew in the opposite direction. He ran as though chased, his mind content to watch his body, the weighty link between them an awful hindrance, happily jettisoned. Colors blended before him, real objects lost their shapes and melted to a collage, a flat abstract design of the world. The picture was pleasing, the colors slippery and infinite. Air flowed through his body as through a sponge.

The first hose he found was lying loose on an area strewn with feldspar ground cover. He wound the heavy plastic over his thumb and under his elbow. The next was set neatly on a rack in front of a small Spanish ranch house. He hefted it onto his back and ran to the car. Laughing, they sped to another cul-de-sac, clearing several houses there, the hoses trickling water behind them and leaving trails on the concrete, puddles in the car. Stillwell drank from a hose mouth as he drove and passed it to Ned. The loose cap tasted of gravel and sour metal. After the third cul-de-sac, Ned realized he was wet. His shirt had broken out in blotchy stains. The back of the station wagon was filled with writhing jungle snakes.

After the fourth cul-de-sac, Stillwell said, "Okay, that's enough." He turned the car and stomped the gas pedal. At home, he eased the station wagon into his own front yard, then revved the engine and crashed through the side yard fence.

Stillwell went to work immediately. He grabbed a hose from the station wagon and ran to the house, twisting one end onto a spigot and unrolling the rest toward the back fence. "You see?" he said to Ned, who stood to one side, not seeing. "You see?" Stillwell grabbed another hose, attached it to the first, and ran to the fence. He fed the slack through a knothole so the open end pointed down the slope. Suddenly, Ned understood. He gathered as many hoses in his arms as he could and carried them to his own yard. There, he did as Stillwell had done, creating green water lines that ran from the house to the hillside. He worked spastically, his breathing moist and uneven. The hoses screwed together roughly in his hands, the threads stripped and rusting. There was no time to test the connections for leaks. When he ran out of outside spigots he removed a showerhead upstairs and attached a hose to the exposed pipe. He had no patience for the window and popped a corner of the glass with his elbow.

Ned assembled eight lines, Stillwell ten. When they were done, the yards were webbed with limp vines, some suspended for nearly the full distance to the back fence. They turned on the water together, hopping the fence to see the first bursts explode on the hillside. It took the hoses a while to come to life, many coughing up air and dirt in violent burps, the lines stiffening under the pressure. Water slicked the steep grade. Stillwell adjusted the hoses to even the flow, and shallow runnels formed.

They climbed to Ned's deck to check the fire's progress. It had crawled to within a mile now, its flames wagging, taunting them like wispy tongues. In a bland moment of clarity, Ned saw how the fire would evade their trap, climb the hill on either side, and creep in behind them, avoiding the hoses altogether. He shared the discovery with Stillwell, who was exploring the fire through the telescope.

"What do you mean?" Stillwell said, looking up from the eyepiece. "I don't understand. What do you mean?"

At nine o'clock, the electricity went, the cutoff abrupt and unannounced. Neither man moved for a flashlight or candle. Heat filled the air and curled the tiny hairs on their arms. Ned could see the fire's reflection in Stillwell's glasses, ragged orange pupils riding the surface of the lenses.

Stillwell stared into the brightening glow. "Vitruvius said language, upright gait, and house building all followed the discovery of fire," he said softly. "Heraclitis said all matter was a manifestation of fire, the common denominator change. When Cabrillo came to San Diego, he saw so many brush fires he called it the Bay of Smokes. Fire is as much a part of Southern California as the watersheds that frame the region. Buildings lost can be replaced, but deteriorated soil, as in Greece or Palestine, is lost forever. We are wholly responsible for this synthetic fire regime, but the pathos and grandeur of a Southern California holocaust makes one think of Dante." He looked at Ned. "They needed a firebreak. We're it."

They went inside to wait. The light of the fire played on the walls, gyrating like smooth ocean shadows. The furniture held them gingerly. Twenty minutes passed in an instant. Ned went to the sink for a glass of water. He held a mug under the tap, but all he got was a dry gurgle. He tried again, jiggling the handle. Stillwell sat up. They ran out back. The hoses were limp, dead. Drying quickly, the ground at the top of the hill had hardened to a crust. Stillwell stepped onto it, breaking through into soft mud. They looked at the fire, huge now and blinding.

$$\oplus$$

Ned turned on the television when power was restored. The sun had come up an hour before, yellow light sharpening everything. Outside, a cool breeze blew and a hawk called. Stillwell lay collapsed on the recliner, eyes staring vacantly at the television set. Forms appeared on the screen, took on color and bulk, resolved slowly into the shapes of men.

A young fireman was being interviewed in a parking lot. His face was covered with black streaks and a metal hat was lodged under his arm. There was a burn on his neck, a large wet rash. Ned recognized the interviewer as the station's weatherman.

"Goddamn, it was hot!" the fireman said. "The smoke was blinding, the roar of the flames was terrific, and you could feel the hills shaking in your feet. Jesus, it was gorgeous, but it sure put the fear of God into you!"

The fire had been out since sunrise.

On the next station, three men in sports coats sat in a semicircle on a small platform. The first theorized that unpredictable winds had pushed the fire back on its own scars, penning it in. The second said the Santa Ana had churned dust and pollen into the air, snuffing it. The third simply shrugged and said it was the nature of fires to die out mysteriously.

Ned turned off the television and watched the colors fade.
Even shadows were bright to his eyes. Deep inside his head,
he felt warmth building, bloating slowly. Stillwell didn't move.
Softly, as though to hide it, he was sobbing.

✚

Ned gathered the hoses from his yard and deposited them
in a metal trash container five miles from home before
Elise returned with the children. She eyed the hole in the
Stillwells' fence when he met her in the driveway, but said
nothing about it or the window he'd broken upstairs. They
unwrapped their belongings and put them away.

He took a week's vacation from work. Elise interpreted
the time off as a sign that he was going to fulfill his part of
their pact after all. Her mood improved. Ned scanned stories
in the paper detailing the damage the fire had caused.
The blaze had been large, but modest compared to fire
complexes up north. The official ignition source was "freak
lightning barrage."

One afternoon, Ned told Elise he might take their son out
to the high school. A game of catch. She was chopping celery.
"Good, that's good," she said.

He found the gloves and his son and left. But instead
of going to the high school he turned north and took them
out onto roads that had been inside the fire, both sides
blackened. The boy said nothing, staring out at the charcoal
landscape. Ned stopped at a dirt turnout and they hiked away
from the car.

It was like a winter scene. All the leaves were gone, but the sparse trees stood firm. The boy found a short branch, miraculously unburned. He used it as a walking stick. As they came up over a rise, a turkey vulture took flight from the ground before them. The huge bird vanished through contrails of snowy black powder. The boy ran down to where the bird had stood and found a dead gopher, burned and pecked apart.

"Cooked meat," the boy said when Ned came up beside him. The gopher lay crouched, as though to wait out something terrible, ants darting in the dry gloss of its wounds. Acid rose in Ned's throat.

He stepped up onto a boulder and looked down into a small valley. The land was decimated. Ball cactus had cracked open like eggs, and there were mounds of twisted still-smoldering palm fronds. Already, green forbs poked up through the scorched earth.

"Die!" the boy called out. Ned turned and saw his son standing like a fencer, jabbing the sharp end of the stick fiercely into the body of the gopher. "Die—die!"

"Hey!" Ned said. He jumped off the rock and grabbed the stick and snapped it over his knee.

✪

Stillwell appeared at the door in a blazer and slacks. He looked out at Ned through eyes laced with red veins, the threadwork magnified in his glasses. Ned stepped onto the porch and shook Stillwell's hand. He had fought with Elise for two days. First about taking the boy to the burn scars, then shifting to the sad taper of their lives. You have six weeks, she'd told him.

"I came over to invite you to dinner," Stillwell said. "My wife's idea. Whenever's good with you people is fine with us."

"How's tonight?"

"Perfect."

Stillwell smiled, stuffed his hands into his pockets, and walked down and around the hedgerow.

Elise agreed begrudgingly. That evening, Ned showered and shaved, drove to the store for wine, and picked up a babysitter.

They walked around the hedge at eight o'clock. The section of fence that Stillwell had driven through had been repaired, new blond wood beside the old brown. Stillwell answered the door and conducted introductions. Throw rugs littered the carpet inside the house, spasms of color and design laid out at odd angles to the walls. Poking from beneath the rugs were slips of ash stains.

"We like it," Stillwell said, laughing. He took the wine from Ned's arm. "We think it's avant-garde."

Stillwell's wife was a short, chunky woman. She frowned. She had roasted a turkey. The thing sat steaming on the table, brown and crisp and still in one piece.

When they sat, Stillwell said, "So, tell me, neighbor, what do you do?"

Ned smiled, and exchanged an awkward glance with Elise. "Well, right now, I'm an attorney. Bankruptcy. How about you?"

"Funny you should ask," Stillwell said. "I'm on severance. They gave me eight months for eight years. It's funny because I may find myself requiring your services."

"I'm strictly corporate," Ned said.

Stillwell grinned. His wife tried to redirect the conversation, asking Elise where the children went to school and who their teachers were. But the talk lapsed to the sounds of fork tines striking plates, fingernails scuffing wine glasses. They settled for silence.

Stillwell broke a minute's lull. "Okay, here's a joke," he said. "What starts with 'F' and ends with 'U-C-K'?" He looked among them all and waited for someone to give the necessary response. "Come on. What starts with 'F' and ends with 'U-C-K'? What?"

His wife exhaled slowly. "What?"

"Firetruck."

He waited for a laugh, but no one laughed or said anything. His face melted into a sarcastic smile as though something unsavory had been confirmed. He pushed out his chair and left the room.

The women stared off at angles. "I'm sorry," Stillwell's wife said.

Ned found Stillwell in the backyard, leaning against a post of a short porch overhang. A drizzle sagged across the night, the world exhaling wet relief. Ned saw lines of ash in the porch floor, streaks of iron in a sandy streambed.

Stillwell turned. He had loosened his tie so that it hung around his neck like a noose. He smiled and produced a small medicine bottle from his jacket. The white pill glowed in his hand. He offered it to Ned, but Ned shook his head. Stillwell shrugged, and set the pill on his own tongue.

They trudged back across the wet lawn. Dinner sat on Ned's stomach as though he'd taken the turkey in whole. Elise paid the babysitter and fished keys from a bowl to take the girl home. "Check the children," she said, yanking the door shut behind her.

Ned pulled himself up the stairs. The children were fine—asleep or faking it. In the bedroom, he stripped and stumbled into the shower. He let the water scald him, run across his body the way he suspected fire itself might: kinky rivulets along his back and between his legs, paths chosen by flame along paper. The wetness and heat created a quieting equilibrium. The hot water ran between his teeth, singeing his gums and tongue. He tasted blood. He dragged his fingernails hard across his chest until the water seemed to permeate him, run into his veins in transfusion. He stayed under the stream until his skin shriveled and cinched.

He didn't bother to dry himself. Naked, he walked out into the bedroom, his body vibrating from the temperature drop. He continued out onto the deck and began to steam immediately in the cold air, white wisps curling away from his arms, collapsing upward and vanishing. He moved to the rail and looked out into the darkness. The sky flickered with tiny distant fires, each a fierce and brilliant burn. He scanned the heavens and looked for pictures among the stars, the geometry of his imagination at work. Then, right in front of him, something fluttered and fell, landing precisely on the rail next to his smoking hand. It was a leaf, a burned leaf. Its flesh was all ash, held together by a veiny skeleton, the fibers twisted and hard. Ned considered the tender gales that had kept it aloft, the pockets of airy protection. He reached out to touch it, and it fell apart.

DOUBLE ENTENDRE

*I don't mean to say that any great passion can exist without a
desire for consummation. That seems to me to be a commonplace and to be therefore a matter needing no comment at
all. It is a thing, with all its accidents, that must be taken for
granted, as, in a novel, or a biography, you take it for granted
that the characters have their meals with some regularity.*
—Ford Madox Ford, 1915

We begin on the sofa. I touch your leg through your clothes. I
touch your lower leg, just above the bone that pushes the skin
from beneath like a tree root pushing earth. I use my index
finger. My skin seizes and my jaw trembles. I move to your
calf, cup its heft. I squeeze and my fingers jog across the skin.
Sexual encounters may be frequent, but they should never be
gratuitous. Emphasize shared feeling. This is romance. Modern
attitudes toward sex should be reflected while reinforcing values
of caring and commitment. Characters need not be in love. Sex
is a wonderful experience. If the erotic story brings a little of that
into the lives of readers then it hasn't done any harm at all.

I open my hand and pass it over your body. Your spine
churns like the silly locomotion of a caterpillar. I pass my
hand across your face, nudge the sharp ridge of your jaw as

though smearing clear the rim of a buried box. The crease of your mouth turns up, and when the lip pulls back I see the gleam of a shiny tooth. I creep around to your nape and the crown of your skull, palming it like a ball. We have begun.

Intimate detail can be employed if it is tastefully done. Clinical phrases are not a good idea. The beginning of an erotic story is in many ways even more important than the beginning of other stories. Get to the crisis as quickly as possible. Sexual tension is to erotica what blood is to sexual organs. Sexual tension is "Geez, he kisses great. Too bad he's wanted for tax evasion in Delaware." Perhaps not all can write erotic fiction well, but every one of us is a sensual being. Good erotic fiction often has a theme beyond the simple mechanics of sex. Get to the crisis as quickly as possible. If characters can't get to the crisis, they should at least get started on the trip that will lead them to it. These destinations are not acceptable: the Middle East, India, Africa, anywhere in the Orient, South or Central America.

We leave at nightfall, a decision made just at dusk, exciting for its suddenness, and twenty minutes later we are on the road, a state highway heading south. The road is nearly empty, lined with farms and country bars whose neon defies the idea of night, fooling insects who orbit them drunkenly in swarms. The curtains of the van flop wildly behind us. You are wearing a long, light dress, but it is pulled up past your knees to let the air in. Men use erotic stories as an aid to masturbation. Women find that racy material increases their interest in sex. On a more basic level, women's erotica tends to be about atmosphere and sensual pleasure that leads to making love, and men's erotica is about fucking and coming.

Erotic fiction is the chance to eroticize anything at all.

We have no destination but the journey itself, its visceral sense of speed and progress as we recede from the familiarity of home. I reach forward and wind the clock on the dash, screw it up. Time doesn't matter. It's June, the third week in June, hot enough to leave the windows open at night, and the humid air streams over our arms, pushing the hairs backward and leaving them bent. The white lines of the road accelerate toward us and fire beneath the body of the van.

How long is this love scene? What are they doing to avoid commitment? Are you writing with all your senses? Conjure the hero. What's it like to have this marvelous man making love to you? Feel his arms, the pressure of his muscled thighs against your quivering thigh. Are your breasts taut with desire? Most human beings have fantasies, and writers are no exception. Most erotica is simply an extension of a writer's own imagination. That said, sexual tension can't last forever—sooner or later, something has to give.

Suddenly, you reach for my hand, pry it from the wheel and pull it toward you. I shuffle to the edge of the vinyl seat. You place my hand on your inner thigh, the muscles there relaxed and terribly soft. You grab my elbow and shove me closer. I keep my eyes on the road, hovering one-handed through the wide play of the steering wheel. I turn my wrist and brush your hair and the skin beneath with my ring finger first. I prod the loose flesh—you are already damp. I concentrate to move that difficult finger, like a painful exercise for piano, and it's not long before the muscle in the back of my hand threatens to spasm. Channels of warmth flood the tiny spirals of my fingerprint, and I adjust to press into your flesh.

You play with my elbow in a way that is confusing at first. Outstretched and hyperextended, the back of my elbow is loose and wrinkled. You tickle me there. The pinches come in pulses, and I realize it's communication, the dots and dashes of a kind of code. I understand it all at once, the way a scholar suddenly understands the all of a lost language. I am to play with you as you play with me. It's because I can't see you—my eyes glued to the moving landscape of the road—that I can translate the touches, submit to your imagination. I don't know if you are moaning or breathing, or holding your breath, so I listen to the warm wind rushing through the fat cab of the van and think of this as your breath, your hot air pressing into my mouth and ears. I move over you. We travel like this for twenty miles, between a town called Barker and a town called Williamsport, until at last you accelerate and dig into the grooves of my elbow so that my whole arm rings for an electric moment, and without thinking I send the charge back to you, eyes locked to the road ahead.

Such scenes are meant to be provocative, but they should be logical too. Most editors don't care if scenes are true, only that they could be true. It's essential to keep track of body parts, and not have vaginas suddenly sprouting from armpits.

It is quite astounding how many men are confused about the position of female genitalia. The clitoris is not situated inside or adjacent to the vagina. If the penis has penetrated the cervix, something very unusual is going on.

Never before in erotica have authors been freer to express tastes. The genre has come a long way. The change began in historical romances. Before, sex was limited to the heated touch, a lingering glance, a kiss on the last page. But then came writers like Rosemary Rogers and Kathleen Woodiwiss. The relationship between authors and readers is like an affair, beginning with a seduction and experimenting as methods stale. Now, anything goes.

You want to take a bath. You light two candles and murmur as you run the hot water. I wait until there is silence before I enter.

In erotic fiction, omniscience is an especially weak device as there can be no withheld information, hence no sexual tension. Additionally, the second person is only rarely used in stories intended for the mass market.

The little room glows yellow. The shower curtain is pulled aside. Her hair is up now, all but for a mesh of downy threads pasted to her neck, and she is immersed in a bath that steams in the low light. Parts of her pierce the white head of the bubble bath, mound islands of buoyant breasts, a sandbar of her belly with the dent of her navel like a hole dug by a child. He steps toward her. For a moment he stares at foam clinging to the wedge of hair between her legs. One thigh is raised and gleams. His first touch is to her breast, spreading the little bubbles so it is like the touch of a million smaller hands. He slides down to her stomach to press her navel, push his finger into its wrinkle where there is the deeper warmth of her body. Her mouth opens and bites itself, teething on her lower lip.

He touches her until the steam fades. She looses her hair, and he feels himself sink and sink. He holds it wet, shiny and heavy, a silky chunk woven with moisture, and he pinches through its pleats, mesmerized by its fabric. The water is cold now, and when she stands she shivers. He pats her down with towels and when she is dry they arrange them into a nest on the floor. He straddles her for a moment, then moves down her body, pausing at each breast to make her nipples rise. He crawls back until his knees touch the cold tiles. He licks at the loose lip of her and he is amazed at how easily she moves. No part of him moves like this. He touches her hard rim, then pushes inside to where she is a delicious singe. He cranes his neck and pries his jaw open. He wishes his tongue were more prehensile. He holds his breath and pushes as deep inside her as he can go, and for some reason, perhaps he believes he can breathe through them, he opens his eyes and scans across the broad expanse of the rest of her, and she is tilted back, propped on her shoulders, and her fingers scrape over his forearms, and her belly stutters her pleasure, and she is lovely in the yellow light.

Are you convinced that the lovers are in love when they tumble into bed? Are you sure you have not been gratuitous? How does he know that she loves him? Can obstacles be dropped momentarily for passion? Have we arrived at the crisis? What has happened to our journey? Be wary of lengthy exposition or description of particular acts. Too much, and your story will stop dead in its tracks.

☩

Much in the same way orgasms can have different levels of intensity, so too can erotic writing. But in writing, unlike orgasms, it's not the intensity of the climax that changes. What changes is the circumstance by which climax is reached. Revel in this, but bear in mind that the average erotic story has two to three sex scenes, each slightly different from the last.

They make the beach before sunrise. The sky is streaked with cumulus. For a while they play in the dunes, dancing, wrestling, waiting for the sun to appear. They hug away the chill of wind and mist blowing off the breakers. The dune grass wriggles a lewd dance, and loose sand blows across the water's hard-packed apron like wispy snakes, drifting snow.

They splash each other to find that the water is warmer than the air, and they strip to march through it naked, treading a carpet of broken shellfish. Low waves strike at their knees, and they dive into them, lips reddening as they fill with blood. She approaches him and puts her hand between his legs. They are waist-high in the water now and he is hopelessly limp. She is amazed at how tiny he has become, and she fingers him like a delicate anemone detached and somersaulting in the waves. She moves her hand to his testicles, cinched as tight as a date, and he feels one of her fingers claw at the tender opening below.

She bares her teeth, clicks them in a flirt. She drops to her

knees, splashing his chest to keep him warm. Then she ducks
beneath the surface of the water to take him into her mouth, the
deflated shaft, the packed testicles, all of it—and it is this thought,
that all of him can be in her mouth, that finally arouses him.

Heroines, femmes fatales, and ingenues are not always low-
class whores. Very often they are high-born whores. But how
many stories about bored housewives can you write? Sooner or
later you're going to have to push the envelope to rich heiresses,
powerful executives, and young people enjoying newfound
freedom. Remember: non-virgins are never seduced. Also,
beware of throwing in sex scenes just for titillation.

She comes up for air, using one hand to complete his
erection. The finger of her other hand enters him below the
water, worming into him. It's only the balance afforded by the
waves that keeps him upright. He feels her knuckle, and then
movement as from something hungry and alive.

He looks up when she goes back under. The sensation is
determined less by friction and rhythm than by pressure
and motion. He feels the soft pillow of her tongue, hot and
working as a guide to her throat. Her finger digs further
inside him, and her other hand molds the clay of his thigh.
The water moves at both her churning and its own.

He looks at the last of the stars, fading, and when he lowers
his head again it appears that some of them have sunk below
the water. But these are jellyfish, palm-sized disks glowing
with internal phosphorescence. Four or five colors drift below
the surface, blues and reds and greens like lanterns decorating
the break of morning. He feels no fear at them. They are simply
alternate beings, fellow creatures, adrift in a cauldron of eggs

and seed. And when he comes, he thinks that they are like the jellyfish, but luckier for this moment of brushing union.

Is this a good time for them to admit their love to each other? Have your characters been making love in character? Is she the only one for him? You're more than halfway to the end, but neither is certain of the actual commitment. Ideas are like foreplay, but actually completing a story is like orgasm. If the story is plausible, the climax will be all the more satisfying.

Note that there has always been a dark undercurrent to passion. We humans tend to prefer our sex a tad scary. Shrewd writers capitalize on this. Hot fiction is real people reacting to a situation that frightens them, pushes their boundaries.

They sleep most of the day on the beach under a blanket from the van, until the sun is descending again. A hundred miles down the road they stop at a diner where the cups don't match the saucers, the forks don't match the knives. Back on the road they see a sign warning against hitchhikers and another that reads LIVESTOCK ROAM FREE. Soon they see the roaming cows, fat and ugly and chewing through the dusk. The roads now have letters instead of numbers or names, and there are no longer divided lanes, just the pavement, and sometimes not even that. They are off the map. The road does not exist. Possibly this is best, he thinks, looking across at her, her hair scrunched at the top of her head in a fist. To map something is to make it smaller, to understand it, and if one can grasp the largeness of the world, its opaque hugeness, then one cannot achieve this sense of being lost, but not lost at all, because lost from what? from home? the world is home, the sky a brilliant ceiling of a vast kitchen, they are surrounded by beauty and bounty and are part of it. He thinks for a time of the hole within him—not like the lingering sensation of her finger, but similar—that he feels when she is not with him. It's a hole he fills with thoughts of her. It's not a hole that hurts, it's not a puncturing, it's a feeling of being lost and found at once, of tolerance and anger and lust and happiness, and of all the most vivid emotions, vivid like colors, discreet in shades, a subtle passage through a spectrum like a sunset, like the sunset into which they now drive.

Unhappiness, discontent, and divorce are the sad endings we all experience, but in erotic fiction we want a happy ending to remove us from all this. Most erotic fiction tends to be sex-positive, so the message is that good sex is something worth having often. Love can be beautiful, awesome in its majesty. To capture a fraction of that emotion is to dance among the stars.

Are we approaching the resolution of the crisis? Are you bearing in mind gratuitousness? The final coming together of hero and heroine should not be mere conjugation. It is consummation—something yearned for by both the heroine and the reader. Erotic stories are about people having sex that is not only satisfying, but also endless. Just as horror stories end with a hint that evil will return, so do erotic stories hint that the sex will go on.

They stop at a farmhouse to ask directions to a motel,
but the fat crinkly gent squints and tells them there ain't
none. He suggests instead the parking lot of an abandoned
Methodist church a mile down the road. He chews some
remnant of his dinner and warns of a local species of
spider—eight hairy legs and a blue dot on its belly.

The church tilts like a bad tooth, and its lot is bordered
on two sides by a flat graveyard overflowing with gothic
monuments, itself walled around with corn still green in the
stalk. Broad and gnarly oaks stand secure among the stones.
He lights a propane lantern and they walk out among the
graves. Many of the monuments are tipped from weather or
the decomposition of the coffin below. The dates are ancient.
B. 1822 – D. 1889. One grave, fallen flat on its back, says only
1658. They hold hands as they wind through the monuments,
and the lantern hisses an answer to the crickets. The corn is
the black wall of a mausoleum.

Back in the van, they climb onto its bed and she wrestles
on top of him and reaches down to guide him inside her. She
has a few ways of this business. One is to execute an aerobic
he can watch, he can see his apparatus—he thinks of it this
way—sinking into her, and another is to ride horizontally
forward and back, grinding their woolly meshes of hair and
secretions. He reaches up to hold her body in his hands,
grab either side of her at the ribs, and she is like a piece of
sandstone, hard, but surprisingly light. She balances on his
chest and squeezes him there, and he wipes at the strands
of hair that cling to her shoulder, and he molds the skin, the
muscle beneath, the bone at the center of her.

She comes down hard on his scrotum. He gasps at what is
not quite the pain of it. As they make love now in a graveyard
he imagines all the other places where they might make
love—cars; racquetball courts; piers; museums; a meadow
where they once chased falling leaves and laughed; sometime
after Chinese food; the beach, reclined against dunes; a
bathroom stall; the mountains, under a misted sky; pressed
against a textured wall; in front of a fire; on fur; on carpeting;
on concrete; in freezing weather, against a tree. He runs his
hand down her flank and up to her leg to work the hinge of
her hip. He is close to coming now, the potential of it fading
in and out. For a time he entertains boyish thoughts of her,
walking together, holding hands, playing games together, the
lower-case tendernesses he would cherish with her. He thinks
briefly of the spider they have been warned of. He's on his
palms, and she's on her elbows, and their legs are crimped
together at the knee, eight tangled limbs, and he thinks *We
are the spider. We are all that is dangerous and beguiling.*

Now she is kissing him, and they are about as much inside
each other as is possible, and this thought is as exciting as
the data transmitted from his extremities. He accelerates
now, and he looks at her closed eyelids to imagine what
she imagines, her parted lips pushing air that shows in the
chill for a fraction of a second, and her fingernails are in
his chest, they feel embedded in his chest, and he senses
tears in muscles all over his body, and bruises forming, and
now he is making noise, he has been making noise for some
time without knowing it, not screams but hard breaths, and
he reaches that point when he knows he will come, that

focal lock in the head of his penis, and now really he need only wait for it, for its sizzle to spread fast across his body in a shot, an explosion followed at once by implosion, and the tension again centers in the head of his cock, and then spurts come flush, like a vein opened by a sudden wound, bursting in concert with his heart, and his warmth begins its swim through her identical warmth, a transfer of life from environment to environment, and as his coming fades and his breathing slows, and she holds him, he knows that he will miss sleeping with her, holding her through the aftermath.

The end of erotic stories may be even more important than the end of other stories. The biggest problem with blending genres is to make the story work in both worlds. The story itself becomes a double entendre. Never forget the six-step story: Boy wants Girl; Girl not interested; Boy makes his move; they have sex; a truth is revealed; the sex goes on.

Has the crisis been resolved? Have you double-checked for gratuitousness? Have you created a convincing Other Man/Other Woman? Have you executed your third love scene?

They sleep for a time, but not long. They wake to a noise outside the van, open their eyes to see the other staring back at them. The sound repeats, just an animal, and he thinks of the way sounds creep into dreams and asks her, "What were you dreaming? Just now."

She looks out the window, into the graveyard. "I think I still am," she says.

A light fog has descended on the church and graves. Its gentle movement gives the world a sense of spin, and a breeze whispers through the corn. There is no sky, and the ground is shrouded as well, and all they have is a flat plane of empty space. They pull closer together for fear, then find it ridiculous. They sit up and stare out the windows. He doesn't know if she's scared, but for a moment he becomes convinced that something will rush from the darkness, from the corn.

"Let's get out of here," she says.

They rush into the front of the van and the headlights flash long shadows that shift and move as the van turns away. She grabs his thigh in fear and they speed off. Three or four miles away it all seems funny. They laugh and when the laughter fades, he tries the radio. He can find only static. They are too far out from civilization yet. There are few lights, and he checks the gas. He looks at her, smiling out the windshield. He sees, just in front of them, a bright star, the polestar. He looks at her, smiling still, content at the thought that they are heading deeper, that they are heading south, that the journey continues. But it's not. It's north, and they are going home.

Is the sex-novel field a good place for a beginner? I'm afraid not. The equivalent today is the mechanical, plotless, hard-core porn novel, composed of one overblown sex scene after another. Any dolt with a typewriter and a dirty mind can write them. But hopefully this turn is only temporary. History will come around again to believable characters. Authors will once again write stirring romances. And the reader, whoever she is, will turn the last page, sigh dreamily, and think *That's the way love really is*.

THE YEAR OF THE DIVA

It was the year of the diva. The song, the Irish lilt, wormed into every knothole. Boomed from lowriders, from radio stations at gyro stands, from the rubber-band clarinet of a street musician who had fingered the melody note by note, from the fat throat of a businessman pissing bourbon and salt onto a paper plate in an alley, embarrassed when I heard him tootling on. First the coarse endearment, then the lusty proclamations, then revival. The song defined the decade. The traffic was monumental. It took the El Niño to shut her up, finally.

The effect, the pattern, the system, descended that year and the weather was screwed up from January on. Sixty degrees on the New Year in China, the spring dead calm. Storm season crosshaired the city with twin fronts, one a Canadian devil surfing down the Midwest feeding on paltry tornadoes and accumulating deaths by flood, the other a rogue hurricane hypnotizing meteorologists with its perfect spiral and sinking two Portuguese fishing trawlers before spotting that other to the west and beelining for it. The city went from summer light to medieval dark in half an hour and what played out overhead was like a sick, sweaty fuck, fat balls of rain pulled to earth, laced with something unspeakable. The power station submerged by six o'clock, highways closed without ceremony. Even the diva was quiet at last.

The wind ripped down the boards, the signposts vibrated as though in the presence of the divine, and lonely umbrellas turned dumb circles on the sand or caught the right batch of wind and ascended right there. The waves dismantled the sandbars and came up under the wood, an aerosol geysering up from splintery gaps, mists like the spume of mammals dying through their blowholes. The storm was the outpouring of the earth's mineral sweat. The rain nibbled faces like a million infectious bats. It teared down the glass, streaked with black. "Acid," said the janitor, from behind his mop's authority. "It's an acid storm."

The storm flooded the city but like everyone else spent itself in three days' time. The shops were all awash, for a while you could canoe through red lights, and when the waves finally pulled back, it took all the touristy crap with it, the T-shirts, the mechanical puppies that yipped and flipped, the key chains, snow globes, decks of cards, slices of pizza, packs of gum, mugs, cameras, ashtrays. It all wound up down the shore with six or seven million clams jostled from artificial beds. Miles of seaweed punctuated the coastline from horizon to horizon. The homeless swooped down to feast beside the gulls.

When the power station came back online, the diva's voice returned and joined them all at the water's edge, the sound track of the world.

THE JOCKEY

In Rattlesnake Canyon, a quarter mile yet from the stables, thirty or so sheriff cars sat parked in a dirt field. Stands of scrub oak and silver dollar eucalyptus walled the makeshift lot, the trees backshadowed by a slice of moon. Matt parked, and we got out. Debbie came to me at once, tying our fingers together in a sweaty sailor's knot. She was spooked. I was relieved because I was spooked, too.

We assembled near the front of the car and looked off toward a silent group of men gathered around an RV painted solid black except for the white letters: SWAT.

"You two ready?" Matt said.

Matt was sixteen, two years older than me. He had a hard corrugated stomach and thick blond hairs all over his arms. He was a Junior Explorer with the Sheriff's Department. He'd been asked to bring a friend along to assist in a Sheriff's Department training exercise: that was me. He thought it would be funny to bring Debbie, too.

I caught him looking at our braided fingers. "Yeah, we're ready."

We set out for the RV and the group of men, but before we got close we were intercepted by Sheriff's Commander Schiff, whom I recognized from the local newspaper. Schiff was tall with a paunch, hair faded to the gray-white-black of granite. He was an unavoidable presence in our town, both because of the converted station wagon he tooled around in and because of the signs planted in front yards every two years that read SCHIFF FOR SHERIFF. He nodded to Matt, and they shook hands. I squeezed Debbie to make up for being left out of it, and fell deeply in love with her when she squeezed back.

Schiff finished an up and down appraisal of Matt, who hoped to be sheriff himself someday.

"I thought I just said you and the one other, son."

Matt craned and squinted to get a better look at the men over by the RV. "They're a matched set. I couldn't get them apart."

"I don't know how I feel about having a young lady along."

"She'll be okay. She's tough."

Schiff looked at Debbie's breasts as though their size would speak to the truth of this claim. They were quite large for her age. "Well, all right—but you're personally responsible, son. Is that clear?"

"Yes, sir."

"Let's head down to the installation."

The installation was a collection of ramshackle buildings, stables abandoned fifty or sixty years before when all the land around here was owned by ranchers. It smelled of old horses and cattle. In previous explorations of the spot, Matt and I had found ancient metal bits, thin horseshoes burning with slow orange rust, and once, a riding crop that Matt had taken for his own and hidden under his bed. We stepped through a break in a wooden fence and approached the complex's main building, a short structure the color of milk chocolate. A man in a khaki safari outfit waited for us. He was just old enough to bald, wisps of hair pasted to his scalp with some kind of gel, and he wore delicate octagonal glasses. He was relieved to see us after all the time in the dark.

"Lenny," Schiff said, "this is Matt, and his two friends. Kids, this is Lenny Dexter, my brother-in-law."

We were all solemn in deference to the task at hand.

Schiff looked at his watch, massaged his jaw in thought. "Okay, here's the drill: this is mock-terrorist, whatever. Matt, you've had sidearm training, so you'll be the perp. That means you'll be role-playing the part." Matt nodded, deadly serious, already in character, and Schiff grinned and turned a half circle in the dirt, reveling in the drama he was about to create. "This—all this—we'll pretend is a racetrack. Yes. Scaled down, of course, but imagine a big dirt track and green infield and bandstands. Lenny, you're the owner, the rich pompous bastard, and you've been abducted by the terrorist. A heist gone bad." He turned to me and Debbie. "You—you're a jockey, here after the day's races. And *you*," he took Debbie's arm and pulled her away from me, stationing her next to Lenny, "you're the owner's wife."

The two men shared a faint sly smile at the joke, which I supposed was at the expense of Lenny's real wife, Schiff's sister. I tried to get Debbie to look at me, to reassure her, but she only stared at the ground.

Schiff continued. "All right, this is what will happen—in roughly eight minutes, Special Weapons will begin a tactical assault on the racetrack. Matt, you are to do everything—

anything—to keep them from taking you or your hostages alive. Don't worry about the guns, they're filled with blanks, and there shouldn't be much firing, anyway. Here." He gave Matt a walkie-talkie from his belt and a small pistol that was really just a cap gun. "We'll stay in contact throughout the exercise. Now listen—about halfway through, something's going to happen. When I give you the signal, you'll let the jockey escape." He pointed with two fingers at me.

Matt nodded, but didn't look like he liked the idea of someone slipping his grasp.

Schiff turned to me. "You'll run like a little mother, all right? Tear on out of there, and when the team catches you, just answer their questions." He swiveled back to Matt. "After that, you're on your own, son. Whatever you want to do. But when I tell you, the jockey goes—maybe even snap off a couple rounds at him as he runs. Understood?" He looked at his watch again. "We begin in four minutes."

Matt hustled us all into the building, gesturing with the cap gun, his finger rested comfortably against its plastic trigger. The inside of the stable was like a public bathroom, a line of stalls on either side with flimsy doors that didn't go all the way to the floor. There was room for maybe twenty horses. The floor was dirt, and the wallboards were warped and cracked from uncountable seasons. Debbie stuck with Lenny, which annoyed me even though she was just playing her part.

Debbie had been my girlfriend for a week. She was from

Kentucky. A strange thing about Debbie was that she had a
tattoo. It was new, and I didn't know what it was a picture of.
She still had the bandage on her arm. She said she wanted
to surprise me when she took it off. I knew only that the
tattoo was blue, because of the ink that came through the
bandage, and generally I thought of a tattoo as a drawback in
a girlfriend. Otherwise, Debbie had blond frayed hair and a
face shaped like a valentine heart. The first time we kissed—
the first time I ever kissed—she dipped her tongue into my
mouth, and swirled it around. I wasn't sure that was right.
Debbie lived in a trailer park, but that sounded okay to me.
Living in a park. I knew that her parents were divorced, but I
didn't know which one she lived with now.

Matt waved the cap gun. "Further in. This is too exposed."

He moved us toward the center of the stable, where we
found a pile of soiled Mexican blankets on the ground, their
colorful zagging shapes faded with the darkness and mud.
Some people believed the stables were haunted, but really
they were just a stop on the underground railroad that
brought illegal aliens from the border to L.A.

"Sit down," Matt said. "And don't make any noise."

We obeyed, and Matt did a quick reconnoiter of the area,
holding the fake pistol aloft as though ready to use it. This
annoyed Lenny, who though he was dressed for it, probably
hadn't counted on sitting in actual dirt.

The walkie-talkie crackled with static, and Schiff's voice
came over the frequency. "Okay, Matt? You there?"

Matt held the radio close to his lips and pushed the
button. "Here."

"You ready, son?"

"Yes, sir."

"All right, they're coming in."

Lenny and Debbie sat across the aisle from me. I looked over at them, and tried to get Debbie to acknowledge me. She refused to look up, trapped in her role, so I stared at her breasts, one of which I had touched through her shirt.

Matt paced above us. "If any of you move," he said, peeking around a corner at the outer compound, "I'll kill you."

Lenny huffed. "Take it easy, kid. It's just a game."

Matt stepped over to him and pointed the cap gun at his face, close enough that if he'd fired, he'd have burned him. "You be quiet."

Lenny tried not to swallow. They stared at one another, acting out a petty confrontation, and Matt gave in first, content to submit as long as he was in control. He strode off to look out into the darkness. It was cooler now, or seemed so. I brought my knees up to my chest, moisture pressing through the butt of my pants. I looked back at Debbie and Lenny, and they were touching at the hip now, sharing heat, but it wasn't clear who had initiated the contact, who had moved closer to whom.

"Debbie," I said. "Come over here."

She looked at me, and then at Lenny, and then at the dirt. "I can't."

"Shut up," Matt said, from the end of the stable. He was silhouetted in the doorway, and I half hoped a sniper would fire his rifle and end the game right there. Matt took a step toward us, freezing when a stick snapped behind him. He paused and dove off to one side, rolling a somersault in the dirt so that he came back upright, cap gun at the ready. We all watched him watch the darkness, slowly rising.

"Hey, pigs!" he yelled. "Come any closer and I'll fucking kill them all!"

He came back to us smiling, pleased with himself, and I smiled back, to make sure he was just acting and that we were still friends. He sneered at me.

"What are you grinning at, you little prick?"

Schiff's voice sounded once again from Matt's belt. "Nice touch, son, but I wouldn't piss these boys off if I was you."

Matt scoffed, and his eyes drifted to one side. He lost himself in thought, watching some version of the next few minutes play out in his mind. He focused on something on the ground beside me.

"What's that?"

I turned my head carefully. Half-hidden in the dirt was an old flat bolt lock, its strange key jutting from the bottom like the handle of a knife used to skewer it. I picked it up.

"It's a lock."

"Give it here."

He snatched it away and stuffed the cap gun into his armpit. He fingered the lock as though it were precious and revealing. Before he could decide what to do with it, Schiff came over the radio again.

"Okay, son, it's time. Send the jockey."

Matt slipped the lock into his shirt pocket, where it yanked the fabric. He pointed the cap gun at me. "Get up."

I stood slowly, brushing dust and dirt from my pants. Both

Lenny and Debbie were looking at me, and perhaps because I relished their concern it didn't seem I had an option not to go through with the escape. Of course, I could have cried and screamed until the illusion was spoiled for everyone, until my parents were brought in to rescue me for real, but by then the scene had grown larger than wants and needs. The trick to coming out of it, I thought, was not to destroy it, but to execute it, to play the assigned role well.

Matt turned his back to me and headed toward the entrance, but I hesitated.

"Can I say good-bye?"

He swiveled about in the dark, eyes angry. "Hurry."

Debbie leapt to her feet and into my arms in just the way I hoped she would. Her breasts pressed against me. After a few seconds, she pulled us apart so that I thought it was over, but then she kissed me, or tongued me, but I didn't mind, it was warm and wet and I felt it working all over me. She finally broke it off, twisting about as if it were too much to watch me go. I took a breath and moved along with my captor.

We walked to the mouth of the stable, Matt using my body as a shield against imaginary bullets.

"Wait until I tell you." I felt the plastic cylinder of the cap gun in my back. "Don't move till I say."

His voice was close to my ear, hoarsed. I wanted to say good-bye to him as well, but the role had changed him. Something had been added or deleted, and I wasn't sure if his pleasure in the game was a memory of a time before I knew him or an emergence. I was afraid to turn and look at him. The darkness of the compound, deep and complete, roused an anxiety in Matt that I felt in his grip on my arm. Off to the right, I glimpsed movement—a hand, I believed, not twenty yards away.

"Three o'clock," I said, to warn him.

"Now!" he said. "Go!"

✛

He shoved me out into the open so that I stumbled and nearly fell, and for a moment I fully expected a cloud of bullets to rip me up. But the volley that came was only three shots from the cap gun, pissed-off little firecrackers sounding as I regained my balance. I ran out of the compound the way we'd come in, arms and legs chugging, strides short and dodging, knowing that at any moment I would be tripped or tackled, then pummeled. Eyes were on me, I could feel their effect, and gun sights. I came to a wood fence I had no memory of, hopped it, and accelerated to full speed on the other side before I thought wait, that fence wasn't there before, maybe I had gone too far, maybe I was out of bounds. I stopped beneath a gnarly oak to regain my bearings, but when I turned toward true north it was into the path of a faceless creature vaulting from the dark.

I hit the ground, and lost my wind when the thing came down on top of me. Suddenly, I was immobilized by a collection of hands, and there were voices, the words recognizable only as questions, to which I had no air to respond. The hands searched me all over, scraping up and down on my chest and thighs. I was lifted to shoulder height, made ever more helpless, and transported a hundred yards beneath the canopy of oak leaves. At last, I was set down and told to kneel, the first command I heard well enough to obey, and I did.

There were lights now, to blind me. I heard a chorus of breathing, and a laugh. Shadows moved in the background, bodies shifting for a view, and presently a figure stepped forward, of something human-shaped.

"Who are you?" it said.

"I'm a jockey," I said.

A softer voice came from the background. "I didn't find nothin' on him."

There was a pause and I realized there was dirt in my mouth. I gathered it up with saliva to spit it out, but swallowed the wad by mistake.

"A jockey. A jockey. You race horses, do you? That's what jockeys do, you know."

"Yes, sir."

"Well, you a good jockey? Bad jockeys cost me a pretty penny. You any good?"

I thought a moment before answering, and there was sniggering all about. "Yeah, I'm good," I said. "The best."

The laughter came again.

"You're okay, you little bugger." The figure hawked something up and fired it into a bush. "Tell me what we're dealing with in there."

"There's one of them," I said. "He has a gun."

"A pistol?"

"Yes."

"And hostages?"

"There's a man," I said, "and a woman."

Another figure stepped forward—I heard his feet move the dirt. "She any cute?"

I paused, hoping I would be rescued from answering this, but there was only the held breath of the men waiting. They shuffled forward, restless.

"She's beautiful," I said.

They quickly began to disperse, full of thrill and motive, and before I knew it I'd been scooped up and was sliding along through the quiet lines of sheriff cars. I looked up and saw it was Schiff who dragged me, his face locked forward as though conforming to some injury to his neck. We descended on the black RV, and he opened the door and pushed me inside.

"Sit down. Be quiet. And don't touch anything," he said.

I was left in the cramped space. I moved inside and looked around. The floor was a dirty plastic tile, the furniture was all attached to the walls, and the windows were high up and useless. Like a cell, I thought. The RV made me think of Debbie's trailer park, the term *mobile home* having broad application in my mind. Now that Debbie was alone out there, I thought, the scenario must have seemed more lopsided: one hostage, thirty perpetrators.

I went to the front of the RV, and tried to see what was happening down in the stables. But it was dark, of course, and lights on in the cabin made a mirror of the windshield so that I got a clearer picture of myself than of the world outside. I was a kid with longish hair, in a sweatshirt a size too large, trying to figure a way to make the night come out right. I loved Debbie, regardless of her blue tattoo. The feeling gave the moment clarity, and that was nice even though the thing that was clear was that I had abandoned her, that I had failed to do the proper heroic thing. I couldn't imagine the how or why of Debbie loving me back. And the vision of myself in the windshield, thinned by the swell of the glass, made me think she'd prefer someone else, Matt maybe, or Lenny, or perhaps one of the men homing in on her now.

I went back to the door and tried the handle, expecting it to be locked, but it was not. Outside, there was no one in sight, but voices came from nearby, transmitting over the radio of one of the cars: "I see him! . . . Where? . . . Right there by that wall. . . . Do you have a shot? . . . No, no, he's moving. . . . If you've got . . . No, he's gone, fuck. . . . Billy, how about . . . Nothin', I ain't seen nothin'. . . . Eggert? Clarke? Cover Billy. Move forward to the tree, son. . . . Moving. . . ." The voices trailed off as though a volume knob had been adjusted, and I looked up at the dry oaks and eucalyptus all around, the hills of a small canyon within the larger valley that held us all. I took a few steps toward the stables. I had no plan in mind—I didn't know where I was going or what I hoped to achieve—but I had the idea that if I at least planned what was right, something wise and just would present itself.

A night vision telescope sat on the hood of one of the sheriff cars, a device as bulky and fat as a Coke bottle. I picked the thing up, rested my elbows on the car, and pointed the lens down at the stables. I put my eye to the rubber, and there was a flash of greenish light, the kind that lurks beneath escalators, and a slow dissolution to a vision of a world entirely other, a glowing dream forest of chill shadow and scampering warmth. I steadied the contraption and saw men betrayed by the heat of their blood, moving between the dark structures of the compound. Inside, I saw pale movement, Matt, bobbing and darting, and Lenny and Debbie down low, so close they were melted together to a single image. The deputies were nearly on top of them. I was too late. At any moment, the order to rush would fly out over the airwaves, and there was no way to prevent it, even if I ran screaming.

The firefight began the moment I lowered the nightscope from my eye. It started with a few muffled cracks from the oaks, and escalated on the line of base human fear. The little white lights were like sparklers in the dark. I didn't find out what had happened until it was all over, the members of the assault team filing past me with their hot guns dragging behind them, their faces grimaced with the knowledge that they would wake in the morning to the memory of this night, and suffer through it again. After a brief but furious exchange, Matt had taken Debbie and Lenny into a back storage chamber with four complete walls and a full-length door. He used the lock we found to seal them in. It was determined that in the four minutes of foolish bumbling it took the deputies to locate and transport a bolt cutter, Matt had plenty of time to fire three shots—one into the heads of each of his remaining hostages, and the third for himself. They found him smirking, the small room clogged with smoke from the cap gun.

I sat in back with Debbie for the drive to her trailer park. I expected she would ignore me, but she slid in next to my leg and spun our fingers together.

Her mobile home sat on wet cinder blocks, the face of it streaked sideways with a broad sunset of rust. The yard was landscaped with gravel and weeds. It was better in the dark, and I was ashamed for having misunderstood it. I let Debbie's hand go, but she grabbed my elbow.

"My father wants to meet you," she said.

I looked at Matt, for whom the night had been a success. He wanted further adventure. He shrugged, and turned off the car.

Inside, Debbie's father sat on a couch watching television. He was a huge fat man. He wore boxer shorts and a tank top, and had hair on his shoulders. His eyes lit when he saw us, and he struggled to his feet and turned off the TV.

"Hello! Hello!"

He waddled toward us, and Matt and I each said our names and shook his bloated hand. His eyes lingered on Matt.

"I know you," he said.

"Little League," Matt said, completing the thought they had been sharing.

"God!" Debbie's father said. "That was years ago. Don't know why I ever did that. But damn you had an arm, kid. I remember that. Well, this is a celebration then! Would you boys like some coffee?" He motioned to Debbie, who moved into the kitchen and uncapped a jar. "Sit, sit."

We moved to where the furniture was, the low sofa with the single heavy depression, and chairs made of vinyl. The trailer was basically one big room. The walls were paneled, the pattern of knots and grain repeating every few feet, and the carpet was a thin retardant shag. I looked around for anything that might explain Debbie's tattoo. Between the couch and the kitchen sat a desk with a glowing computer, the keyboard covered over with papers. This was strange, and Debbie's father caught me looking.

"I write romance novels," he said, and there was a pause that even Debbie observed from the kitchen. Her father glanced between Matt and me, and laughed. But the laughter didn't seem to mean he was kidding.

Debbie brought us three mugs on a waitress's tray. Mine was hot, and I rested it on my knee.

"Ah, yes," Debbie's father said, taking his cup in both palms. He sipped immediately. "Thank you, dearest. The coffee bean. That's why we killed those crazy Brits! Drink it black, boys. That's the only way."

Matt slurped up some of the coffee, and smiled. I raised my mug to my lips, but just blew into it. I hated the stuff.

"There you go," Debbie's father said.

Debbie came to my chair and stood behind me. I could feel her looking over my shoulder at my cup. As though she could read my mind, she reached down and took it, moving it to an end table.

"Come on, I'll show you my room," she said.

Her father lifted his eyebrows at us. "Sure, sure. You kids go. Matt and I will have us a little reminiscence here. Men and their beans!" He backhanded Matt's knee, and for a moment the two of them wore the same pleasant expression. Debbie's father winked at me. "Watch out for that girl. She's got the same genes as her dad."

We had to leave the mobile home to get to Debbie's room, which wasn't a room at all, but a hitch trailer for camping. Parked behind the house, it was silver and old, the corners rounded for wind resistance when it was on the road. Debbie led the way inside, and turned on a light with a thin hanging chain. A bed was covered with dirty laundry and a small sink brimmed with bowls and mugs. The trailer tipped just so to the right.

Debbie cleared a space on the bed so we could sit. She draped her arms over me at once, and put her mouth to mine, her tongue pushing through my lips. It wasn't unpleasant, though, and I felt my body trembling.

We lay back on the mattress. I moved my hand down her chest, brushing over her breast so that I could say for sure I'd touched it twice. Then I moved to her wrist and brought my hand back up her sleeve, stopping when I ran across the wrinkle of her tattoo bandage. Pressed right to the skin, it was hotter than the rest of her.

She pulled her face away, and moved to unbutton her shirt. I grabbed her fingers.

"No," I said. "Don't."

She looked back and forth between my eyes, and smiled nervously. "I had a nice time tonight." She took my hand and moved it between her thighs. "Touch me here."

I heard Matt and Debbie's father laugh at something in unison. Debbie kissed me again. I exhaled into her mouth. I didn't touch her between her thighs. Instead, I raised the sleeve of her shirt until her tattoo bandage was exposed. I ran my finger over the seam of it. I smelled infection. Debbie looked at me and bit her lip, and nodded. I peeled the bandage away.

UTOPIA ROAD

They came to Utopia Road when there were no olive trees, no lawns, no ice plant hillsides; they came when it was a blacktop street and tiered lots the color of grocery bags, when the sidewalks were white and even the sewers were new. They came when the foundations had been laid, driveways cut into the curb, addresses assigned. Up and down the street, families gathered on the concrete slabs of their living rooms, waving to one another as if to attract the attention of someone in a plane. From station wagons and rented cars they watched muscled men erect spindly sculptures from piles of two-by-fours. Soon, they could discern the style of one house from another. Spanish, ranch, colonial, Victorian. The more curious crept around the houses on lots adjacent to their own, peering up flights of winding plywood stairs, invading the Sheetrock rooms into which they would eventually be invited. Sod, stacked like jelly rolls, arrived on trucks with high metal walls. Trees, eucalyptus and acacia and palm, appeared overnight in the ground near the street. They watched from a distance as tiles and shingles were set delicately in place.

Water rushed through underground pipelines, passing through filters and sieves in distant windowless buildings. Electricity was generated in automated power plants, crossing deserts on suspended cables. Both moved in swift currents. In a week, the toilets flushed, the spigots ran, and the garage doors opened automatically. The tall cement streetlights stained the air yellow when dusk fell on the electronic eye of a black metal utilities box at the top of the street. The construction workers cleaned the houses of bent nails and tar paper, swept away plaster chips and sawdust, and then rode off on the beds of aging pickup trucks.

They moved to Utopia Road on a three-day weekend. Arriving in a caravan of family-sized vehicles and brightly colored moving vans, they carried into the houses upright pianos, overstuffed chairs, and boxes marked FRAGILE in stenciled letters. They formed lines and passed along lamps, garbage bags stuffed with winter clothes, garden hoses, and milk crates filled with kitchen appliances. They worked through the night, replacing darkness with the trained headlights of a dozen minivans, the streetlights adding a dim yellow sheen from a distance. When it was over, they collapsed on quilts and afghans and carpets yet to be stained by their timid pets. Families slept together, limbs overlapping. They barely breathed and no one snored. The Gibbs family came out of it first, rising together in the late afternoon and stumbling to their driveway. They pulled plastic outdoor furniture from the garage to the sod lawn and sat, sore and stunned from sleep. Awakened by the movement, the Springers next door came outside as well, following the sound. The families introduced themselves and listened to their stomachs growling. The fathers left to find food and came back with chicken in red and white paper buckets. Others woke now to the smell of the meat and walked up the street, as if strolling or merely exploring, and joined the group on the sod lawn. The Shalladays, the Haysletts, the Dautremonts. The new neighbors ate and talked and laughed. They exchanged phone numbers, made plans for dinners and card games, and did not notice when the streetlights flickered on around them.

The men spread shards of bark where there were no plants to hide the natural light brown dirt, and neglected the timed sprinkler systems they'd paid extra for. Their wives planted gardens and fed tropical fish papery multicolored flakes. The children stood together at the bus stop in the morning, dew wrinkling the pages of their schoolbooks; the boys drove go-carts made from particleboard, the girls talked to themselves and their dolls.

Water ran through the houses like blood, the slim plastic pipes a system of veins and arteries. It sat in freezer trays in crescent shapes and hung loose in the air on chilly mornings. Electricity was channeled to the houses, spinning through fisted mats of wires in the black utilities box. The neighbors tapped into it through wall sockets that looked like pairs of small excited faces. The electricity sang, blended, cooked, compacted, and spoke. When it was used up it vanished entirely.

For several months, static ran through the air and gave the neighbors sharp shocks when they touched metal or each other. Small weeds that sprouted in the seams of the sidewalk gave Utopia Road a lived-in look.

✚

The Royces, the family in the corner house, became the subject of hushed discussions. Mr. Royce, a hulking crew-cut man, failed to return the casual waves of the other men, and Mrs. Royce became infamous for throwing the dead bolt of their front door so that it made a whip-like crack. On Utopia Road's first Halloween, the Royces posted a sign on their stoop: DO NOT RING BELL. Rumors spread that Mr. Royce was partially retarded and a veteran of the Bay of Pigs and that Mrs. Royce was a bankrupt fortune-teller and an agoraphobe. Their only child, a boy named Tom, was the sole teenager on Utopia Road, and though he was not as reticent as his parents (he used the street as a runway for his fleet of remote-controlled airplanes, the children following him in packs), he was quietly discussed along with them. Fathers told tales of being anonymously strafed by miniature Cessnas, and mothers claimed to have seen him standing over injured boys in the street. Tom denied the aerial attacks, claiming he no longer owned a plane like the one described, and the bruised sons always took blame for their wounds on themselves. Tom was a dark boy, even his eyelids and armpits were tan, and he was thin, efficiently built, muscles like ropes under stretched skin. Most of the mothers were secretly attracted to him, considered him handsome and manly even at sixteen, and several, under the strained hum of a vacuum cleaner, played

with the idea of seducing him for an afternoon. Sleek as a
skink, Tom wandered up and down Utopia Road cocky and
bare-chested. He took up smoking shortly after Easter.

The mailboxes of Utopia Road were small-scale replicas
of the houses that loomed behind them. The carrier was a
kindly, gray-haired man named Mr. Rapp. While delivering
Mother's Day cards and get well notes to the small model
homes set on posts at the ends of the driveways, Mr. Rapp
beamed at finlike palm fronds shifting in the breeze. He
walked carefully across layers of red pumice, pausing
frequently to feel the bark of a tree or pity a blue-belly lizard
flattened on the asphalt. Utopia Road was his favorite part of
the route. One day, while he was delivering a small brown box
that smelled faintly of yeast, Mr. Rapp was struck by an odd
thought. He looked around himself, saw sheets of tiny purple
ice plant flowers, frail heads of birds-of-paradise, a sinister
ivy clinging to a salmon-colored stucco wall, and realized
that everything he saw had origins in other parts. Everything
had been brought here from somewhere else. Cement, seed,
metal, plastic. Mr. Rapp was thrilled and saddened at being
an abrupt witness to the capacity of man. He let the package
that smelled of yeast fall to the ground and looked up and
down, focusing on nothing. He touched himself in several
places as if he had misplaced a pair of glasses.

Someone put a cherry bomb inside the mailbox in front
of the Gibbs house. Shards of plywood scattered in the air

when it blew, and the burnt husk of the model home fell in the street. They couldn't prove it, but the neighbors privately held Tom Royce responsible for the explosion.

On the Fourth of July, they barricaded the end of the street with red, white, and blue painted sawhorses and decorated trees and fire hydrants with crepe paper streamers. They brought outside long tables and sun-faded beach umbrellas. They ate food they had carefully prepared and wrapped in plastic. They held events for the children—a bike race, a water balloon toss, a miniparade with a patriotic theme—awarding construction paper ribbons to the most talented or best dressed. The men were pleased when Tom Royce, who had watched from a distance for most of the day, signed up for the afternoon Ping-Pong tournament. Unfolding three Ping-Pong tables on a level part of the street, the men nudged one another, pleased to have this opportunity to put the boy in his place. Tom drew the only bye in the first round. After ten minutes of stretching, he won his second-round match easily, forcing Mr. Holderness's shots into the nylon net with a clumsy-looking combination of English and slice. In his next two matches, he made the ball skirt off the table at gross angles by incorporating an odd high-toss serve; distracted by their wives teasingly rooting for the boy, Mr. Springer and Mr. Bohnenkamp couldn't keep the spastic ball in play. Tom helped himself to plates of lasagna and potato salad as the men huddled in a group and discussed strategy for the finals. Mr. Gibbs received advice and warnings. Mr. Holderness swore that Tom had appeared in two places at once to return a pair of smashes. When the final match was played, Tom switched playing styles altogether and wedged his paddle between his index and middle fingers like the Olympians. He beat Mr. Gibbs quickly with a wicked tight-arched backhand.

Dejected, the men awarded Tom the stiff blue ribbon and completed several unwatched consolation matches in the quirky glow from the streetlights. Tom pinned the ribbon to his belt, sat on the electronic eye of the black box at the top of the street, and watched the neighbors gather their belongings and ornaments. Later, while the sky filled with flowery explosions, the men complained to their wives about the sudden animation in a boy normally withdrawn and laconic.

Mr. Gibbs is working near the free-form carp pond he had installed in May, pulling tall weeds that have the pond under siege. On the weeds' stalks are curving clawlike spines that inflict wounds that swell and ache. He has pricked himself several times. He stands above the weeds and pulls with the muscles in his back. The roots make muffled popping sounds and come up in his hands. The carp, red and white and tan, avoid the activity, swimming in tight circles on the other side of the pond. After re-moving each weed, Mr. Gibbs takes a breath and surveys his yard.

At first, he thinks the sound is an insect, a house fly or honey bee. From a distance, from the ground, it has that kind of report. He grunts and swats behind his head, concentrating on the careful placement of his hands. It approaches until it makes the sound of an alarm clock, an oven timer. Mr. Gibbs pulls another weed and wonders who is running a lawn mower in his yard. He lifts his head and holds his breath. Hydraulic fan, he thinks, chain saw. He is struck on the back of the neck and the force throws him. He hits the ground with half his face. When he opens his eyes he sees the small wrecked plane on the other side of the pond. Wings broken, grids of wood exposed along the fuselage, a softer electric razor sound coming from the gas engine. Mr. Gibbs can just make out the Windbreaker and the sunglasses of the small painted pilot in the cockpit. The carp nip at bits of cloth and balsa wood floating on the surface of the pond. Delirious, Mr. Gibbs tries to purse his lips like the calm fish. There is his neck, his face, sharp points of pain in his hands and forearms, and a tiny click as power to the plane is cut from somewhere nearby.

They woke to find the rain gutters torn from their houses. Some of the metal lengths hung precariously from the eaves, joints hyperextended; others had been stripped completely and lay on the ground in Z shapes. They felt the smooth crimps in the aluminum with silent amazement, and searched their yards for footprints or animal tracks.

"It's Tom Royce," Mr. Gibbs explained. He reached back to the base of his skull and touched a row of metal staples that ran like a zipper down his neck. "It's him, I swear to God."

When night fell, the men gathered in front of the Royce house. Several brought long-handled garden tools that they held like weapons. They shined flashlight beams in the windows and called for Tom to come outside. After ten minutes, they spotted the distorted neon glow of a cigarette dodging behind a pane of clouded glass near the front door. When Mr. Gibbs threw a rock onto the roof, Tom appeared and faced them from the upward slope of the driveway. They shined their lights in his face.

"I didn't do it," Tom said. "It wasn't me."

"No?" Mr. Gibbs said. He stepped forward, turned, and parted his hair to show his shaved neck and the row of metal staples. "Well, how about this?"

Tom tried to speak but stuttered. He looked left and right, then broke for the door. Mr. Gibbs caught him by the foot, and Tom fell on a brick path. Leaping on top of him, Mr. Gibbs pounded his fists and elbows into the boy's body. Tom fought back meekly; the rest of the men only watched. When they heard a bone pop, Mr. Shalladay and Mr. Oberholser pulled the combatants apart. The boy collapsed and lay motionless. Mr. Gibbs paced excitedly and peeked around the shoulders of the men who held him at bay. Tom reached up and covered his right eye with both hands. He stood slowly, and shuffled toward the house. When he'd disappeared, Mr. Gibbs laughed and cleaned a brush wound on his arm with saliva.

A yellow FOR SALE sign appeared in the Royces' front yard

the next morning. It stood as though marking a grave. The neighbors called the number printed on the placard, and marveled at the low asking price. The ranch house with an intercom system and a flat ceramic cooktop sold in a week and a half to a family named Moore.

The Royces moved immediately. The neighbors watched from the shade of the Springers' screen-enclosed porch, drinking iced tea and commenting on the three figures hefting a grandfather clock into the back of a moving van. The Royces loaded a rifle case, two pool tables, a basket from a hot-air balloon. A player piano, three antique metal mannequins, four identical televisions. When the van left they filled their car with potted cacti and Styrofoam wig heads. Before driving off, the Royces took a moment to stand at the base of Utopia Road and stare up the street. Reclined in their seats, the neighbors refused to move under the stiff gaze.

When the Royces' car rounded the corner, Mr. Gibbs sipped from his glass and looked at the faces gathered around him. The staples on his neck had been removed, leaving a squiggly pink scar and a dusty layer of stubble. "Now things can get back to normal," he said.

In the morning they found their pets dead. Legs rigid as tree branches, animal faces tight and strangled. Some were found floating in swimming pools, others huddled in the dark corners of garages.

"Poison," Mr. Gibbs told his wife. "He poisoned them somehow."

They buried the animals in shallow graves, under trees that had been losing leaves. They marked the spots with crosses made from lumber, the pets' names written quickly in pencil against the grain of the wood. The children pressed their palms against the mounds of disturbed earth.

✚

Lightbulbs burst in their sockets. Bits of roofing fell to the ground like rotted fruit. Small geysers appeared periodically where sprinkler heads had broken off, and they found windows shattered mysteriously. One afternoon, the cathode-ray tube of the Bohnenkamps' television exploded, spraying the family with small bits of glass.

A week after the Royces left, a rumor spread that Tom had been sighted behind a row of split-leaf philodendron. He had a wrench, the story went, and was doing something to a spigot. His bare skin appeared slightly gaseous, not quite solid, and he didn't bob his head or make a sound when he moved away.

✚

They lost power. The cutoff came one night at dusk, preceded by three staccato surges. Their first instinct was to jostle the wall switches, play with the on-off mechanisms of their machines. They went to the fuse boxes and found them unchanged. When it was fully dark, they visited one another and were comforted by a sense of mutual crisis. Only the streetlights were unaffected, the yellow light casting a bleary pall over Utopia Road. The neighbors lit candles and spaced them through the dark houses. Families congregated and watched the colored wax melt away.

In the morning, the men gathered around the black utilities box at the top of the street. They searched the metallic surface for whatever damage Tom Royce had caused, touching it gently as if moving it might inflict further injury. Crouching, several men placed fingers on the box and peered into the electronic eye as if it were a microscope. They saw only the eye, opaque, the size of a sand dollar, looking back at them. The men guessed at the problem and at whom to call to fix it. They considered taking the box apart, but could find on it no screws or clamps or bolt heads. A few of them lined up on one side of the box and tried to tip it, but it was no good. They stood confused for a time and then retreated home.

The faucets went dry—they cut into water lines and found chalk dust in the pipes. Rafters made splintering sounds at night and carpet curled on itself like sun-beaten paint. Plaster peeled off the walls in soggy strips. The Haysletts' house shifted on its foundation: they could see it tilting slightly to the right when they stood in front of the mailbox and compared the house to its tiny replica.

Mr. Springer dug a pair of shallow trenches from his pool to the independent Jacuzzi near his house. Using two trash cans outfitted with wooden fins, he rigged a waterwheel system. The water ran down the trenches, spinning the trash cans and a long dowel rod connecting them. A rubber belt linked the rod to the shaft of a small turbine generator. The water gathered in the drained Jacuzzi and was siphoned back up to the pool. The system provided enough energy for a few low-watt bulbs in the Springers' house.

✛

Late one night, they held a formal meeting to discuss their alternatives. Some wanted Tom Royce arrested, others thought they should take the law into their own hands. When Mr. Gibbs suggested that they find the Royces and firebomb their new house, several neighbors shouted approval and stomped their feet on the floor. "That won't do any good," one wife hollered over the ruckus. She claimed to have just that night seen Tom flying down the street—arms spread and toes pointed. The neighbors voted to call in a specialist.

Mrs. Bohnenkamp remembered seeing an exorcism ad in the classifieds of magazine. She dug the slick out of a pile in the garage and called the number listed there. The exorcist was a Native American named Laughing Coyote. Mrs. Bohnenkamp heard the click of wooden beads through the phone. The neighbors gathered money for the fee.

A small delegation met Laughing Coyote at the airport. The group stood pressed together as if posing for a picture. Coming down the jetway, Laughing Coyote was not hard to spot. He had stiff gray hair that hung to his shoulders and skin the color of a house brick. He wore faded blue jeans and a large silver belt buckle. Unprompted, he walked to the group from Utopia Road.

On the way home, the neighbors explained that their ghost, their apparition, their whatever, was not a dead person—he was still alive and presumably living nearby. They related some of the boy's antics. They told Laughing Coyote that stars could be seen through Tom's liquid form. The old Indian watched the land wash by and said good words. He made their problem seem typical and easily solved.

Laughing Coyote told them to park at the base of Utopia Road. When the car stopped, the Indian got out and moved quietly across the asphalt. The neighbors followed. Laughing Coyote stopped on a manhole cover and squared himself with the road. Glancing from a scrub oak that had fallen across the sidewalk to holes where stucco had begun to crack off the houses, he stared at Utopia Road as if he were thinking of buying it. There were twisted garage doors and patches of tan dirt where the sod grass had shriveled and disappeared. A mass of witchweed attacked a privet hedge. Laughing Coyote sniffed the air and cocked his head as if to listen to the water rushing beneath him.

Finally, the old Indian stepped off the manhole cover and approached the neighbors. He gave Mr. Gibbs their money in an envelope and got back in the car.

The Detweilers moved within a week. It took them eight hours to load their belongings into a rented truck. The others stood by and watched, kicking lava rocks loose on the uneven sidewalk. Mr. Gibbs grabbed Mrs. Detweiler's arm as she hurried by with a drawer full of utensils.

"What are you doing?" he said.

"We're leaving. We're jumping ship." She nodded to the place in the street where Laughing Coyote had stood. "I know a sign when I see one."

"That guy was a fake. Cowboy boots, string tie. He was a fraud."

Ceiling material flaked away in chips, revealing cottony pink insulation. Rotted walls broke apart like clods of dirt. Sidewalk sewer openings crumbled away, leaving gaping holes in the street.

The Oberholsers left at night, said good-bye to no one; the Holderness family abandoned everything they could not fit into their station wagon and hatchback. Others moved formally, sweating it out until the scheduled date. The remaining families stayed inside. For heat and light they burned wooden hangers, bits of furniture, cardboard, family files. They sat in groups and spoke infrequently. They stopped sleeping in their beds.

The Springers got lucky. A single man whose job was bringing him west bought their house sight unseen. The man said it was more an investment than an actual living space. The Springers took the first offer and paid three points.

On the morning of their move, the Springers sat quietly on their front step. The air was still and thick. After a long wait, a yellow moving van turned onto Utopia Road. It executed a

complex turn at the top of the street and stopped in front of
the house with squealing noises from the air brakes.

The Gibbs family crossed the street slowly, a shuffling group.

The two families and the movers loaded the belly of the
van. Sheet-wrapped furniture, knee-high stacks of framed
pictures, boxes that had once been Christmas presents. The
Springers left behind mattresses that tore and fell apart
when they tried to disassemble them. The movers bolted the
doors of the van and left for the new house.

The two families stood around the Springers' minivan.
The children looked at one another strangely, twisting their
bodies on rooted feet. The women hugged and wished one
another good luck, and the men shook hands. The Springers
climbed in their car and idled down the street, waving until
they vanished.

Late in the afternoon, Mr. Gibbs waded knee deep into the
pond in his backyard and tried for half an hour to grab the
slick dodging carp with his bare hands. It was nearly dark
when he got a metal-headed rake from the tool shed and
gaffed the cream-colored fish from the shoreline. Beached
on the wilted grass, the carp wiggled back and forth, quietly
suffocating. Mr. Gibbs cut the plastic handles off a jump rope,
ran the frayed cord through the fishes' gills, and carried them
into the house. Mrs. Gibbs laid the fish out on a cutting board.
She cut off the heads and tails, boned and gutted them, and set
the fillets in a frying pan. She took them back outside to where

Mr. Gibbs was starting a fire, using dry twigs and flint stones from his youngest son's rock collection. When he got a spark they both blew on it until a flame caught a leaf. They got the fire going and took turns holding the pan over the flames.

"It's going to rain later," Mr. Gibbs said over the sound of the fish. He jerked the pan so the fillets shifted position.

"Yes," Mrs. Gibbs said. She took a deep breath and looked up. "Look at the moon."

They ate inside, dividing the fish into five equal portions. Alone on the plates, the carp looked barren, slightly unhealthy. The family sat on the floor in a circle and ate with their fingers. When they finished, they wiped their mouths with the backs of their hands and plucked rubbery bones from between their teeth. The children cleaned the dishes with pond water and replaced them in the cupboard.

They bedded down in the living room, putting on jackets and scarves. They wrapped themselves in blankets and pressed their bodies together. They unrolled thermal sleeping bags and hid in the diffuse glow underneath.

They had no clocks, no watches that worked. They did not know what time it was when it started to rain. The sound woke them and they rose, groggy and disoriented. The air was warm and moist from their breath. They listened to the rain pelting the roof. It was dull sounding, a rumbling, the first perception of a distant stampede.

Mr. Gibbs retrieved a large rubber mallet from behind the sofa. He stood, resting the mallet on his shoulder, and looked at his wife.

"I'll check the windows."

She nodded and tended to the children.

Mr. Gibbs went upstairs first. He had boarded all the windows that had shattered or collapsed and on these he rechecked his work, feeling around the edge of the planks for moisture. He inspected the nails. When they weren't tight he choked up on the mallet and tapped them into place. The rain made a different sound against the wood. Deeper and muffled, like knocks on a hollow box. The wind howled outside. Mr. Gibbs stopped his work and listened. When it faded he could hear one of his children, the youngest probably, sobbing downstairs. His wife was saying, "It's only the wind. Don't be afraid. The wind can make noise sometimes. . . ."

Mr. Gibbs tightened a screw with his fingernail and finished the upstairs rooms. He came back down and went into the kitchen, pulling the curtains across the sliding glass door. He rehammered a few nails in the boards over the sink. In the family room, he shut the flue of the fireplace and examined one of the few remaining intact windows. After jostling the panes with his fingertips to see that they were secure, he looked out at Utopia Road. The scene was dark and wet. The street, near the curb, was a river. There was white water near the gutters. Lit by the flickering streetlights, a section of wooden fencing floated downstream like a raft until it caught on an abandoned car. Mr. Gibbs moved closer to the window and set his hands on the sill. He felt a dizzying coolness. He thought, *I'm thirsty*, and the raindrops came horizontally, splattering themselves against the glass as if they were trying to get at him.

THE HISTORY OF RIDDLES

I take the box to the table where we will be playing later in the evening, once the Samuelsons arrive. The box is sealed. It's an informal rule that the host couple provide a new board and pieces for each match. Some people have taken to burning the boards after their games, Frank says, and on top of the housecleaning he has unwrapped a wax starter log and yanked open our flue. Now Frank is dusting. He's on the prowl with a feather duster and a moist paper towel folded into a triangle. The house looks as good as it has since we moved in, but Frank believes dry dusting causes motes or whatever to become unsettled and once they have resettled the surfaces need to be gone over again.

He walks by me to a mote gathering place. "You can open it up," he says. "The cards are sealed again on the inside."

"Really."

"It's just for show. No one would ever cheat. Actually, you can't cheat."

"You can't."

Frank stops. He can't say what he's going to say and keep moving at the same time. "Primitive tribes held contests for justice in the archaic days. The outcome kept the peace among parties in dispute." He shrugs. "The ethic of the game doesn't allow cheating."

Frank has been talking like this ever since the game reeled him in, coming out with lines he's memorized from its literature. We picked up our board this afternoon at the mall. The shelf was looted when we arrived, and Frank just about panicked.

"Jesus," the store's stock boy said, at how quickly the boards had vanished.

"And just two short months to Christmas," I said, wry.

The boy rolled his eyes and trudged back to the stockroom for more. Another couple was waiting by the time he returned, a couple not so different from Frank and me, probably preparing for just the kind of evening we had planned. At the register we all fell in line together.

"Who are you playing?" the woman said. She was nestled into her husband's armpit, holding their board like a cake box. She was just being chatty because the girl at the register was slow.

"We're hosting the Samuelsons," Frank said.

The woman's eyebrows hopped. Her husband did not flinch except for the tiny motion of pulling his wife slightly tighter to his side to comfort her.

"It's an honor the Samuelsons have agreed to play us. They're quite talented," Frank explained in the parking lot. He added, "You know, it's the play factor that produces the fundamental forms of social life."

The box is the size, I imagine, of a million dollars neatly wrapped and stacked. On its front is what the game's enthusiasts, Frank now among them, call its crest, a kind of double-bulb shape playing on the gender icons and the symbol of infinity. The crest is a not-so-subtle pitch to couples, and it seems to have worked. The edges of the box are clasped shut with stickers that are smaller versions of the crest, gripping its seams.

"Go ahead," Frank says. "Open it up."

Matches take place at night. Our girls are already in bed. In the quiet of Frank's dusting I think I can hear them breathing down the hall. They sleep with their peach pit mouths wide open.

"These Samuelsons," I say. "They know what they're getting into, right? They know we've never played before."

Frank cocks his head to scan the memory banks. "Play cultures are hard to tell from what anthropologists call 'phratria.'"

"Phratria. Like fraternity."

"Exactly." He smiles. "What is the fun of playing? Play assumes elements of beauty. The Platonic association of play with holiness elevates the concept to the highest regions of the spirit. Go ahead, open it up."

He sounds like a monk. He eyes me for a moment longer, and turns to a set of our wooden blinds with his moist triangle, which reduces mote disturbance I suppose. I look at the box. I don't know much about its rules, but Frank has assured me it's really quite simple. When the game first appeared people bought boards as presents or party gags. Families huddled around coffee tables at night to roll the queer dice and answer queerer questions. Not even Frank was interested, then. We tended not to care much for the world outside our home. We had the girls and our marriage, and it was all habit enough. Frank believes youthful misjudgment accounts for what's become of our union. He thinks of it that way. He doesn't know why, but we've both turned out differently from what either of us would have predicted years ago. I think another way. What I think is that the world's accelerating mood and the sacred chore of our daughters set us on paths subtly divergent, and we didn't notice until it was a gap impossible to span.

The game didn't need us. The crest appeared on billboards with no explanation attached, and some kid spray-painted the symbol on a cement underpass near our home. I heard strategy on the whispering lips of women in the supermarket, and Frank heard tactics in the flamboyant boasts of men killing lunch hours in locker rooms. A social network formed around the game as neat and efficient as a secret society. I thought of it alternately as a Ponzi scheme—those scams that told you which of your neighbors were really your friends— and a subversive political movement, a weirdo worldview gaining steam at torch-lit meetings. As interest in the game fell into orbit around couples, I began thinking of the matches as séances, Ouija deviance that would soon go the way of the hula hoop. But it didn't, and the literature of the game soon followed, self-published pamphlets of history and instruction and advice, all delivered in the brainwashy tone of self-help. When Frank came home one day with a mouthful of dogma, I realized we no longer live in a world where it is possible to remain ignorant of that which becomes popular. You either go along, or be thought troubled, abnormal, diseased. I agreed to the Samuelson match—Frank arranged it through a work contact—but to be honest I didn't know what to expect, and I was a little afraid. Would there be robes and chanting? Would we all wind up holding hands? After we let them into our house, would this Samuelson woman, this stranger, pull me aside and whisper that my husband was handsome, and what did I think of hers?

✪

We painted over the spots where the girls had crayoned the walls. At night, the line between old paint and new paint can pass for shadow. We washed the windows because grime shows better in the dark, and we pushed aside our curtains so that our neighbors saw into our home for the first time in months. Frank arranged two closets and all the crap under the sink. It was the kooky discipline of the game that the house be orderly, not just look it. We vacuumed and shampooed the carpet. We mopped and waxed. We dusted meticulously, together, washing our knickknacks and figurines as though prepping them for cute surgery. And now Frank is dusting again, eyeing me as I reach for the box and pull it forward.

Something smells like a pine tree, I think, but it's not a pine tree.

"You're nervous," Frank says.

I shrug and finger the edge of the box. Something inside has heft to it.

"Listen," Frank says, "when a child plays a game, he plays in complete—you can even say sacred—earnest. But he plays and knows that he plays. This is the main characteristic of games. Seclusion. A game is played in one time and one place.

It contains its own meaning. Play begins, and at a certain moment it is over. But while it is in progress all is movement, change, alternation, succession, association, separation."

Frank runs a roofing company. He puts roofs over people's heads, manages others who do so. Sometimes he participates in the labor himself—he's that kind of boss. How he has changed is by becoming dissatisfied with this simple provision. A thing about Frank: he wears his emotions on his sleeve. He's never learned to hide them, which is what I do when I look at my husband now and wonder who he has become. His eyes are earnest and his speech is pleading, like a young man articulating politics to an impressionable lover with the hope that she will adopt his view, return his passion. A few months ago Frank tried to interest our girls in softball—another game. But they disappointed him, and he skulked and lamented not having a son. Now, he uses the feather duster to articulate his words, ticking them off like an orchestra conductor calling for notes, and dust motes break away from the synthetic feathers and escape again into the room, radiating off like heat, like an aroma.

"Whatever happened to 'It's not whether you win or lose . . .'" I say.

"The Dutch have another saying. 'It's not the marbles that matter, but the game.'"

I give the box a little shove. "Explain this to me again. There's a board, right? And pieces?"

"Yes," he says. "But that's only one aspect. The dice and tokens simulate insignificance and the fickle tease of nature."

I am nonplussed at this. He frowns. "Look, the contest as
one of the chief elements of social life has always been
associated with the Greeks, right? Yet there was no transition
from battle to play in Greece. Instead, it was a development
of culture in playlike contest. Roman society couldn't exist
without games. They were as necessary as bread. People
had a holy right to them. Civilization is rooted in play—in its
absence, society is impossible."

He's so enthusiastic, I let him think it's sinking in. "What
are the other aspects?"

His eyes shimmer as he rushes to the table to sit beside me.
"You mean the questions."

"Yes."

He presses his hands reverently, laces his fingers to a
thoughtful double fist the size of a cauliflower.

"What do you know of the history of riddles?" he says.

"Absolutely nothing."

"Do you know the sophists? Have you heard the enigmatic
questions posed in Vedic hymns?"

"You know I haven't, Frank."

"Child psychologists have found that a large percentage
of the questions posed by six-year-olds are of a cosmogonic
nature. Were you aware of this?"

"The thought had occurred, yes."

"The riddle is an important part of social custom. It
branches out in two directions—mystic philosophy and
recreation." He pauses and purses his lips. A dust mote sails
by us, but Frank doesn't see it as he settles into a channel
of thought. "What makes water run?" he says. "What is

dead? Which came first, night or day? How many heavens are there? How does God sit on his throne? What is the difference between the souls of the damned and fallen angels? Is the earth solid, or are there holes? What makes seawater salty? What are the causes of volcanic eruption? Why do the dead evidently not desire to return to earth?"

He looks at me as though he has just completed a homily.

"I don't know how to answer those questions," I tell him.

He grins. "That's just it. No one does. The game isn't who gets the answers right, it's whose answers are *better*."

It doesn't make any sense. But still I smile, as there's reason for smiling. It's the first time in as long as I can remember that Frank and I have talked of anything that isn't the girls or the roof or the house. My husband speaks to me of ancient Rome and magic puzzles. He wants me to be happy too, and he looks at me with a variation of desire. He's here, he's dusting. It's all like it was once, when we stood on the same plateau and our world was not rent by variety of experience. To return to that, I'll answer any question you want.

Frank covers my hand with his hand, long enough so that his heat becomes my heat. Then he winks and flies off to tidy rooms the Samuelsons will never see.

I peel the crest stickers back carefully. It doesn't seem right to tear them. The lid of the box eases off like fitted mastercraft, the decompression of air an illusion of hydraulics. Inside are the smells of fresh product: cardboard dust and new plastic.

The board itself is on top, wood with three hinged sides. It settles flush on the table as I unfold it, crushing a crumb we have missed. I trace a few of the hexes. They are inlaid, teak or cherry, and the seams are varnished and imperceptible. It will be a shame to burn it later. Next are the question cards, in plastic like lunch meat: rip to open and a watertight seal for later. There's a separate velvet-lined case for the tokens, little detailed figures carved from that same teak or cherry, each with a felt butt and all so pretty they could enact their own scene of the Nativity. Then there are the dice, what Frank assures me are the genuine ankle bones of Central Asian sheep, the chance devices used by early monotheists to divine the will of God. At the bottom of the box is what the game has by way of instruction, a small book bound like a children's story, on its front the arcane crest again.

Frank closes a door down the hall. I hear the tick of the clock, and look at it. The Samuelsons are due in twenty minutes.

The first few pages of the book are pictures. Egyptians in profile hunched over ancient game boards, panels of poofy-dressed Renaissance men crowding chess, a nineteenth-century masterpiece of a well-to-do mob in frenzy about a roulette wheel. When the text begins I recognize Frank's metered tone. The game spirit of archaic times began with a gift-giving custom called the potlatch, the book claims. The potlatch was held in conjunction with feasts celebrating births, deaths, marriages, tattooing, whatever. If you were a chieftan who went to another chieftan's potlatch, your gift to him, for the sake of honor, better well be grander than his to you, and you were pretty much obliged to throw a potlatch of your own. The gifts started out as practical items that floated between tribes, like a sweater that didn't fit anybody. But before long the custom took a bizarre turn. Clans destroyed items of value as gestures of superiority. One chieftan burns a pile of blankets, another trashes a canoe. One kills a few slaves, another slaughters even more. The spirit of the potlatch, the book says, appeared in scholarly work on Greek, Roman, Old Germanic, and ancient Chinese traditions, and it was the potlatch that gave rise to the agonistic decisions of our world, where who wins becomes who is right, who is just, who is ordained.

Frank emerges from our rooms. He steps out the front door to bang his hands together, applauding away the dust that has stuck to him. He comes back inside, caresses my neck and shoulders as he passes by. His knees crack as he stoops beside the fireplace to get the starter log going. I walk to him. He strikes a match and the flame sucks to its low harmonic. He strains as he rises and pulls me into the crotch of his shoulder, and together we watch the log ignite.

"Baby," I say, "is there any chance that we're supposed to have something for the Samuelsons?"

"What do you mean?"

"Like a gift," I say.

"A gift?"

I kink my neck. "A bottle of wine. A fruit basket."

I feel him tense beside me, a bulge of panic. But he won't let the thought out his mouth.

"No," he says. "We're the hosts."

He waits for me to say more, tugs me against his side when I am silent. He steers us to the window. It is just as our breathing aligns that the Samuelsons' car appears, drifting down our street like a helium balloon as they scan for addresses.

"'Let the young men now arise and play before us,'" Frank says. "Samuel, Book Two: 2:14."

He waves a hand over our heads as the car stops at the curb. The headlights go out, and now we can see the two profiles sitting side by side. The Samuelson woman lowers her visor to check her makeup. Mr. Samuelson waits patiently, then climbs out and walks around to release his wife. When she emerges, she first passes him a box, and even in the dark, even through our vague flickering reflections, we can see the ribbon around it, a pretty facsimile of a flower.

"Oh," Frank says.

We ease away from one another as the Samuelsons approach. I look to our house, neat for the first time in years, quiet but for the hum of the fire and the sleep of our far-off children, and I wonder what of ours could we destroy to prove to these Samuelsons that we are worth their while.

✚

There's a powerful relationship between play and opiates in our brains, the little book said. *They're called neurotrophins. Play strengthens connections between neurons, and makes us more intelligent and fit—more successful adults.*

The Samuelsons are successful adults. They are handsome, a decade further on. If we're supposed to have something for them, they don't show it. They're quite talented, after all.

Mr. Samuelson looks like he's been bald most of his adult life, and Mrs. Samuelson has the easy confidence of women who've come to terms with middle age. They split and assault us by gender. The men shake hands and smile as they discuss Jim Gallagher, the contact who made the evening possible. Mrs. Samuelson thrusts her gift at me and announces, "This is only chocolates, dear, but please don't open them until we've gone. I just can't."

We steer them into our house for the obligatory compliments, which arrive promptly. Frank heads for the fireplace to add logs.

Mr. Samuelson trails him. I hear him say, "There's nothing like a nice blaze in a comfy home."

Mrs. Samuelson makes for a photo of our daughters, asks their names. "Mr. Samuelson and I have three, but now they're grown and gone, grown and gone," she says, tsking.

It's odd that the house is so suddenly full of life. The Samuelsons move comfortably about, robots with precise instructions, but I notice each of them subtly checking on the position of the other, like divers connected by a tether. They are comfortable apart, but reluctant to leave each other's sight.

"Play is more original than civilization," Mr. Samuelson announces, each word a truth demanding confident expression. He and Frank have turned their discussion to the game, and Frank is attentive in the manner of an acolyte. "The game represents a contest for the best representation of something. The contrast between play and seriousness is fluid. The game lies outside morals, values. It is neither good nor bad. It can only be enjoyed as a social fiction in which two groups stand opposed, but united by a spirit of hostility and friendship combined."

Frank nods, basking. I send him a telepathic message to offer the man a drink, but he doesn't hear it.

"Psst!" Mrs. Samuelson says. She has moved to the kitchen without me, and, smiling, repeats the hiss and curls a finger to call me toward her. I tense as it's the odd moment I've feared, but I am drawn across the floor as surely as a paper clip to a magnet. She catches me by the elbow and pulls me close.

"Something in here smells like a pine tree," she whispers.

I crumble inside and smile. "Well, I can assure you it's not a pine tree," I say.

We giggle like girls, then make drinks for our foursome.

"Opposed groups contend for the pleasure of parading superiority," Mr. Samuelson says, taking bourbon from his wife. He and Frank back off a step so that the four of us form a diamond pattern before the fire. "Munificence for the sake of honor! For the sake of outdoing your neighbor! Technology made communication easy for mankind, and intercourse promotes the competitive spirit, but I'm afraid commercialism just does not belong to the immemorial play-forms. Therefore, every man and woman should play the noblest games and be of another mind from what they are at present."

"Bravo," Frank says, and the men click their glasses and drink.

We stand in the fire's heat and crackle, and Mr. Samuelson lifts his wrist to check the time. His watch face glints orange.

"We should prepare," he says. "It's nearly time. The finer players—this is a new wrinkle—have begun timing matches so that we're all playing at once. Everywhere. It's a nice touch."

"Quite," Frank says, and extends a palm to move us all toward the table.

We take our places, partners opposed.

"You started without us," Mrs. Samuelson says, of the mess I've made of the box's contents.

"I hope that's not—untoward," I say.

She sees she's unsettled me, and pats the table between us with three healing fingers. "Not at all, dear," she says. Then she traces the gridiron. "What a lovely board."

Mr. Samuelson slips a collection of papers from behind his lapel. He arranges them on the table before him. "Just a little housekeeping," he says, licking a forefinger. "Now Jim Gallagher—that forgetful old rat—he never told us your rank, exactly."

He looks at Frank, who smiles as though it's the beginning of a joke in which he must participate.

"Our rank?"

"Yes. I need it for the paperwork. We could do it later, but that makes more paperwork for the ratings folks. And really I prefer to do things"—he reaches across to tap the game's thin tome—"by the book."

Now Frank sees it's not a joke. His smile evaporates. He stares at Mr. Samuelson until the older man squints back at him.

"Is something wrong?"

Frank doesn't move. The terror is plain on his face, but still he tries to contain it. He doesn't fear losing. He fears not playing. I wait a moment for him.

"We're not—ranked," I say. "This is our first match. We thought you knew."

Now Frank snaps awake. "We're quite ready. We've been preparing for some time. We could simply begin."

The Samuelsons have already locked eyes. They don't say anything for a time.

"Is there a phone?" Mr. Samuelson says.

"Yes," I say, and rise to escort him to where it hangs. He dials quickly and turns toward the corner to make a private booth of his body.

Frank places his palms on the table. I eye his jaw. He glances away as I return to my chair. Mr. Samuelson makes his connection and begins speaking with the light tone used for business unfortunate but perhaps amusing. His words are muffled.

"This isn't your fault," Mrs. Samuelson says. "It's happened to us once before."

"I don't understand why we can't just deal and begin," Frank says.

Mrs. Samuelson sighs and grins sadly. "Mr. Samuelson works very long hours. It's only rarely, these days, that he can escape for an entire evening. It'll make sense when you are no longer provisional."

Frank swallows audibly. I want to reach for him. But there's no time for it, as Mr. Samuelson is striding back to the table, heading not for his chair but for his wife, stepping in behind her to place his palms at her elbows and help her up.

"There's been an error," he says. "That Jim Gallagher—he mixed you up with someone else. Or us. But we've figured it out now, and there's still time to make the night right. We must hurry."

We all rise and move to the door, accelerating as toward the center of a vortex.

"The couple you were supposed to play—they're on their way here now," Mr. Samuelson says. "They have less experience, but great promise, Jim says. And he knows, that rat. These pairings make much more sense for everyone. Perhaps you'll start off your career with a victory. Wouldn't that be encouraging? Well, good luck and goodnight."

Mrs. Samuelson glances back once at her pretty box of chocolates. It would be easy enough to offer to return them. But I don't. I only smile and reach for the door, and now we have the gift for whoever comes along next. Mr. Samuelson is oblivious and pulls his wife to the car, and we watch until they climb inside and speed away.

Frank sobs, just once. He cries like a man, slow and reluctant, and when I notice he tries to rush away. I tie him in my arms. He relents and presses against me, his body convulsing as though to buck the sadness.

"Life has become a game of culture," I say. "The ritual form persists, but the religious spirit has flown." His pulsing stops now so he can listen. They're not my words, of course, they're from that little book, but I realize it's the language he may understand, so I am happy to use it. I squeeze him tighter and speak into his shirt. "Why does the baby crow with pleasure? Why does the gambler lose himself in passion? Why is the crowd roused to frenzy around the football match? Play may be deadly, yet it remains play. So now, my husband, wake and tend our fire, for our opponents will be here shortly."

ABOUT THE AUTHOR

J. C. Hallman grew up in Southern California. He studied
at the University of Pittsburgh, the University of Iowa, and
Johns Hopkins University. He is the author of two books of
nonfiction, *The Chess Artist* and *The Devil Is a Gentleman*.
He lives in St. Paul and can be reached through his Web site,
jchallman.com.

ACKNOWLEDGMENTS

I'd like to thank the editors of the following magazines, whose generosity and wise counsel gave these stories their first voice and shape: *Tin House, Boulevard, Manoa, The Antioch Review, Prairie Schooner, Fifth Wednesday Journal, Ecotone, The Greensboro Review, Willows Wept Review, Great River Review, Exquisite Corpse, Other Voices,* and *Beloit Fiction Journal.*

As well, the following works proved indispensable in the production of these stories: *Fire in America,* by Stephen J. Pyne; *The Normal and the Pathological,* by Georges Canguilhem; *The Varieties of Religious Experience,* by William James; and *Homo Ludens,* by Johan Huizinga. I'm particularly grateful to Lynn Margulis for permitting me the opportunity to disseminate, albeit in unusual form, the seminal theory she first described in *The Origin of Sex.*

Thanks, finally, to my agent, Devin McIntyre, and my editor, James Cihlar, who is just one of the many good people at Milkweed Editions.

MORE FICTION
FROM MILKWEED EDITIONS

To order books or for more information, contact Milkweed at (800) 520-6455 or visit our Web site (www.milkweed.org).

The Farther Shore
Mathew Eck

Ordinary Wolves
Seth Kantner

Roofwalker
Susan Power

Driftless
David Rhodes

Aquaboogie
Susan Straight

The Blue Sky
Galsan Tschinag

Montana 1948
Larry Watson

MILKWEED EDITIONS

Founded in 1979, Milkweed Editions is one of the largest independent, nonprofit literary publishers in the United States. Milkweed publishes with the intention of making a humane impact on society, in the belief that good writing can transform the human heart and spirit.

JOIN US

Milkweed depends on the generosity of foundations and individuals like you, in addition to the sales of its books. In an increasingly consolidated and bottom-line-driven publishing world, your support allows us to select and publish books on the basis of their literary quality and the depth of their message. Please visit our Web site (www.milkweed.org) or contact us at (800) 520-6455 to learn more about our donor program.

Milkweed Editions, a nonprofit publisher, gratefully acknowledges sustaining support from Anonymous; Emilie and Henry Buchwald; the Patrick and Aimee Butler Family Foundation; the Dougherty Family Foundation; the Ecolab Foundation; the General Mills Foundation; the Claire Giannini Fund; John and Joanne Gordon; William and Jeanne Grandy; the Jerome Foundation; Constance and Daniel Kunin; the Lerner Foundation; Sanders and Tasha Marvin; the McKnight Foundation; Mid-Continent Engineering; the Minnesota State Arts Board, through an appropriation by the Minnesota State Legislature, a grant from the Wells Fargo Foundation Minnesota, and a grant from the National Endowment for the Arts; Kelly Morrison and John Willoughby; the National Endowment for the Arts; the Navarre Corporation; Ann and Doug Ness; Ellen Sturgis; the Target Foundation; the James R. Thorpe Foundation; the Travelers Foundation; Moira and John Turner; Joanne and Phil Von Blon; Kathleen and Bill Wanner; and the W. M. Foundation.

MINNESOTA
STATE ARTS BOARD

NATIONAL
ENDOWMENT
FOR THE ARTS

A great nation
deserves great art.

TARGET.

THE McKNIGHT FOUNDATION

Interior design by Steve Foley
Typeset in Lino Letter Roman
by Steve Foley
Printed on acid-free Glatfelter paper
by Versa Press, Inc.